Flop Shot

An Ooze Owens Mystery

JACK HOWLAND

JACK HOWLAND

DEDICATION

For the friends with whom I've golfed. In no particular order they are Travis, Ki, Gus, Ned, Craig, Jon, Andy, Coalminer, Matt P. (whose head I nearly took off), Travis's dad (Jim), and brother (Tyler).

For those friends who don't golf. In no particular order, they are: Bill (for his unflagging allegiance to PGM), JBC, CPG, MTF, KMR and Sam-and-Alex (whose contempt for the sport I've always admired).

For my boys, who are both good boys, the record should show, but who don't enjoy playing the game as much as driving the cart.

JACK HOWLAND

ACKNOWLEDGMENTS

I'd like to thank my friends and family, naturally.

I'd like, as well, to thank the various pros, courses, and driving ranges behind my game's vertiginous ascent (or descent?) from the low-100s to the mid-90s.

CHAPTER ONE

A nice golf club on a summer night is a deeply sinister thing. Sure, it may not look that way. You may arrive along some winding lane. You may bob and weave through the rainbow spray of irrigation guns. Perky young women (or young men, I'm not here to judge anyone) may flit about golden fairways in tiny skirts, to the trill of laughter and tinker of cocktails. And yet it's all a trap. Like a dynamite cigar. Or a rake in the grass. Or Little Big Horn. I'm not a smart man, and at times I say things that don't make sense even to me. But I say this with perfect confidence: a nice golf club can be as terrifying as any blimp disaster, if circumstances thus conspire.

I said as much to my caddy, Giancarlo Scillaci Buonorotti, as we made our escape from the Sennetts Harbor Club, that of Sennetts Island (Maine) and the venue of this most recent series of atrocities.

"That was terrifying, Buonorotti!" I shouted. I was driving my convertible and had to shout. I usually drive. Buonorotti is Italian.

Buonorotti nodded slowly for about an entire minute.

"Yes," he said, also slowly. "Yesss, is true, Oose."

"I mean, I thought I was a dead man!"

"Indeed, my friend, you did almost die."

"Ha!" I contributed. "HA! I almost died on several occasions!"

His arm slung over the car seat, he merely turned a wrist in reply.

"And then in the middle of it," I continued. "Wink Freaking Paddington shows up! In freaking Maine!"

"Yes," Buonorotti observed.

"To jam me up!"

"Who can know the motives of a man such as Paddington?"

"I can! They're bad!"

"Your fates are entwined, Oose."

At that very moment, we drove off the island and onto a causeway. I pressed down on the accelerator nonetheless, the full moon racing along with us, behind the pines, as if unwilling to let us go. The cartoon maiden on the "Come Again!" sign filled my mind with visions.

"Golf is a demon goddess, Buonorotti!" I gasped, building on one of his general themes.

"Is very true, Oose."

"Like some gorgeous, deranged, ex-wife," I continued, almost trance-like.

"Very much so."

"... Godzilla-sized, breathing fire, wearing this kind of molten, glowing bikini and popping golfers' heads off with her thumbs!"

"Golf is indeed a beautiful demon, Oose," Buonorotti said. "One who has cast a cruel spell over both of us, over many millions. Leaving us humiliated, broken, ruined."

"Don't I know it!"

"Her spell is still on us, Oose," he added. "This we cannot forget."

"How could anyone forget!"

"And yet, I have traveled the world, lived a long life, and seen many things ..."

"You were a high-class gigolo!"

"And I do not believe that there is anything more exhilarating than to steal the love of this cruel and beautiful Demon Goddess of Golf."

"Me, neither, buddy!"

"Which you did," he said, dropping his glasses to his nose. "You ravished a goddess, Oose."

"Well ..." I blushed.

And to imagine that Buonorotti and I barely knew one another at this point!

In any event, we did escape the Demon Goddess of Golf, if only for a moment, and that's the important thing.

So before I get too far ahead of myself, I should clear up that my name is U.S. Owens. That's short for Ulysses Slayton Owens. "U.S." to some, mostly friends. "Ooze" to others, like my three ex-wives, various relatives, and the general party of detractors I've acquired over the years.

The provenance of "U.S." involves the general and president, Ulysses S. Grant, and the Mercury astronaut, Donald Kent "Deke" Slayton. My mother greatly admired Grant. My father, also an astronaut, lost a bet to Slayton. Still, both parents liked how it worked out. They were proud Americans as well as Army brats, so they understood the effect of a great name when it came to service advancement. As my mother once said (around a long, menthol cigarette): "'Armstrong' and 'Buzz' got to take one giant step for mankind. 'Michael Collins' got to keep his cracker ass in the Orbiter." It was undeniably true that my father, Rupert Valentine Owens, kept his cracker ass in the proverbial orbiter his entire career. His name almost certainly was a problem. The gambling didn't help either.

I am primarily or at least spiritually a golfer. I travel the country playing tournaments, not unlike an errant knight, but living out of my (father's) 1970 Plymouth Fury III convertible. I have but one purpose in life: to regain my PGA Tour Card. It's an arduous, expensive and generally humiliating process.

While spiritually a pro golfer, I am professionally a private investigator. Apart from simply needing the money, I do this job because (a) I fell into it, (b) it's super flexible, which allows the golf to happen, and (c) I discovered that, when I've angered a client or investigative subject to the point where they want to kill me, I play golf on a level achieved by perhaps a dozen other people in the history of the game. You can re-read that sentence, if you'd like, because it's kind of important. Luckily, I should add, I arouse clients and/or subjects to this murderous state not infrequently, as private investigation is mostly about divorce. And, in most divorces, at least one of the divorcing parties is prepared to kill any number of people, even those only peripherally involved in the proceedings.

I had just such a divorcee lined up for the Sennetts Harbor tournament. In fact, the ex-husband in this case, Auchincloss Hastings Burr, was easily the most dangerous ex-husband I ever managed to attract, and as such, there was perhaps no ceiling for my game.

When a husband's out there hunting me and I'm playing out of my mind, I do nevertheless have a weakness. I'm not too proud to admit that. I play like a god with my woods, irons and wedges. With my putter, however, I'm like Superman in Bizarro World. Up is down. Left is right. Fast is slow. Which is to say, it's not merely that I can't read greens — rather, my greens-reading gyroscope seems to spin in directions counter to actual physics. My greens reading is so bad, in fact, that other golfers stop me to ask where I'm aiming, purely out of a certain morbid curiosity. So without an exceptionally gifted greens-reading caddy, I'm helpless.

To address this failing, I'd hired Harry O'Brien to haul my bag at the Sennetts Harbor Tournament. Harry couldn't read a course book to save his life and I'd learned to consider his shot-by-shot guidance a kind of comic relief, but he could sorta steer me around the greens. And Harry could also swing an iron at an approaching husband with the very best of them. Together, over a series or tournaments, we'd clawed our way back to the top of the semi-pro ranks.

Really, this was it. A shot at the title. A big win at Sennetts Harbor, and I'd requalify for a Tour card. Well, I'd qualify to qualify. I won't bore you with the details of how that works, largely because I don't understand them, but having been on the Tour and won, I could skip to the head of the line, so to speak. Harry and I had talked excessively about it. Or rather, in retrospect, I talked, and Harry nodded with his one pinched eye. So this was it: we'd gotten back to the threshold of golf Valhalla, the PGA Tour. We'd done it together. Me, terrified by various former clients into playing otherworldly irons and woods. Harry, like Edgar to my King Lear, leading me around the greens.

Which made Harry's betrayal all the more shocking. I remember it like it was yesterday. It was in fact just a few days ago, Wednesday morning. But the real significance of that morning was that I met the aforementioned Giancarlo Scillaci Buonorotti for the very first time.

In any event, we'll start the story on Wednesday.

CHAPTER TWO — WEDNESDAY

I rose early that Wednesday morning, practically bristling with optimism. Harry and I shared a room, my finances being what they were. As such, I very quietly snuck out, discovered a beautiful New England day, and skipped down to the motel lobby. Returning with two coffees and a paper, I found Harry already up, dressed and packing his bag.

"Harry?" I choked, the facts being plain. "You're leaving me?"

"I gotta call for a Web.com gig in Long Island," Harry answered, without even looking up. "A gig that pays real money."

"Real money? How much real money?"

"A lot more than we could win here," Harry said. "And I won't have to fight some seven-foot lunatic with a black belt and a trust fund."

The seven-foot-trust-fund lunatic to which Harry refers here is the aforementioned Auchincloss Hastings Burr.

7

"But, Harry, we're about to qualify for the Tour? We'll make a buttload of money on the Tour!"

"We're about to qualify to qualify."

"I know! Isn't that great!"

"You qualify to qualify. Then you gotta qualify some more."

"That's right! For the PGA Freaking Tour!"

Harry showed me that pinched eye, then resumed packing.

"And Burr isn't seven feet," I snorted. "He's like 6'5"!"

"Right."

"That's barely six feet, Harry!"

"Uh-huh."

"You're like, what? 6'3"?"

"I'm 5'11."

"5'11"? No! C'mon!"

"I'm 5'11, and I'm old," he said, zipping up the bag and throwing it over his shoulder.

"You look great, Harry!"

"And, frankly, you're too old. Just how old are you, Owens?"

"What does that have to do with anything?"

"How old?"

"I don't know!"

"48? 49?"

"My game is in its twenties!"

"Golf is gay enough without the Peter Pan element."

"I have no idea that that means. Who's going to read the greens? I'll be blind out there, Harry!"

"Find another caddy at the club."

"There are no caddies at the club!"

"Because you guys don't pay anything. Which is why I'm leaving."

He started for the door. I blocked him.

"I gave you everything we ever won, Harry."

He looked at me.

"Which was $1,200. We coulda made ten times that if we put a little money on ourselves."

"Gambling demeans both of us, and the gentlemen's sport of golf. And a great democracy!"

"Right," Harry said, then added a tight smile. "You're okay, Owens. But you're entirely delusional. This can't go on forever."

He pushed me gently aside. My mind raced.

"So let's go down swinging together, Harry!" I said, seizing his shoulder. "One last tournament! One last psycho husband! It'll be our last stand! Harry and Ooze! Back to back! Husbands coming at us from every direction!"

"Sorry, Owens," he said, detaching my grip.

He clattered down the steps. I followed.

"But what if Burr attacks me? He's like seven feet tall!"

"Go for his knees," Harry said over his shoulder.

"His knees?"

"Go for his knees, Owens. With an iron."

Car door. Car engine. A quick salute, and Harry was backing up. My mind flickered.

"Which iron, Harry?!" was all I could think to ask.

He rolled down the window.

"The two," he said, humoring me, starting toward the street.

I watched his Buick Skylark take a right onto US 3 and into traffic. I stood there, helpless.

"You always say the two!" was my bootless cry.

It was a beautiful summer morning, I should emphasize. A couple fluffy clouds preened through the sky. Seabirds and regular birds made their various tweets and peeps. A dewy kind of presence filled the air, but somehow felt healthy and encouraging, in a way that dewy things, in my experience, rarely do.

The point is that it must have been the gloriousness of the day that inspired me to persevere. Hope springs eternal, or at least did on that Wednesday in Maine, and great morning weather helps. I took a deep breath (two parts sweet summer air, two parts smoldering parking lot). There was nothing to be done but race to the club and snag whatever caddy I could.

I scampered back up to the room, grabbed my clubs, scampered back down and threw them in the backseat of the Fury. I started the car, let it roar its fearsome morning yowl, then took off.

Today, I'd play a practice round. Just like a tour event, this tournament would proceed over five days. Wednesday, a practice round. Thursday through Sunday, rounds one through four. A cut on Friday afternoon. That format is a rarity on the semi-professional circuit, it should be noted, as club members are generally unwilling to give up so much course time. Not so the Sennetts Harbor Club. Undoubtedly, they had an eye on hosting a tournament for the Web.com, Hooters, or, heart be still, PGA Tour.

On two wheels, I took the loop around Sennetts Harbor itself, a sparkling bower of enormous sailboats, enormous motor yachts and a couple token lobster rigs. The harbor came and went, and I banked the Fury hard left. I blew through the stone gatehouse in a cloud of dust, then gunned it to a far corner of the lot.

Turning off the engine, I pulled my hat and chin low, shrunk down in my seat, and made a 360 scan of the environs. I had to operate on the assumption that Auchincloss Burr was everywhere. With no Burr in sight, however, I emerged, slung up my bag, approached a tree, and took another discreet survey. All seemed well. Burr, in all likelihood, was still asleep.

I followed a screen of privets toward the tournament table, just off the clubhouse patio. I set an exploratory toe out into the highly visible cart path. It was right around this moment that a voice boomed out from the heavens, and my vertebrae briefly separated and rejoined like shuffled cards.

"OWENS!!" the booming voice said.

It came from behind the tournament table and belonged to one Hank Vaughn. Hank was a lifer on the tour admin side, and we'd known each other for years.

"Shut up, Hank," I hissed, hopping over to the table as if on hot coals.

"Great to see you, Owens!" Hank bellowed. "Gonna hit some balls? Get warmed up? Hey, everyone, Ooze Owens is here!!"

Hank, I now noticed, had hearing aids the size of tangerines in his ears. I strangled out a smile.

"Hank, if you don't mind, I'm trying to keep a low profile."

"Oh, sorry. It's these crazy hearing aids," he roared, pointed and grinned. "Another husband out there on the prowl, Owens?"

"Yeah, well, listen, Hank, are there any caddies available today?"

"Ha ha ha!"

"Yes, Hank, I actually didn't mean it as a joke. I need a caddy."

"Ha ha! Wait, you're serious?"

"Yes, so are there any around?"

"Not for you semi-pro cheapskates. They all disappear. You know that!"

"DANG!" I said, and meant it. I should point out here that I never swear. Like my ban on gambling, I resist bad language both on superstitious and moralistic grounds. There was a time, I'm not too proud to admit, that I worked in obscenity like a prodigy. However, I soon noticed a correlation between my cursing and rough play, and thus 86'ed it.

"Can we call some of them?" I asked.

"Yeah, but they won't come. See these Maine caddies usually work multiple jobs," Hank continued, tucking his thumbs in his belt. "A little looping here, a little lobstering there, maybe some taxidermy, maybe homemade fudge."

"Homemade fudge?"

"So it's easy for them to up and disappear. Ha ha ha! What?!"

A different voice, somewhere offstage behind a stack of programs and other detritus, repeated something.

"What? WHAT? Oh? Oh? Oh, really?" Hank said, turning back to me and hitching up his buzz cut. "Actually there is a caddy."

"Great!"

"He's from Italy."

"Fine."

"Never seen this course in his life!"

"So what!"

"Bonjourno," we both heard, then turned to see a figure in the shadows of the tent.

I remember the sun moving briskly behind the clouds. I remember light coursing over the lawn, igniting motes of dust like little fireworks. I remember, finally, the shadow in the tent coming toward us, then a wall of blinding sunshine, a clap of thunder, and then — so help me God — in a single, shimmering sunbeam, Giancarlo Buonorotti.

His jaw was like a block of concrete. His shoulders filled the horizon. If he were a horse, he would have been the winged variety. He would have reared up, rolled his mighty hooves in the air, and given a deafening neigh.

"My name is Giancarlo Scillaci Buonorotti," he said. "Like the greatest artist and the greatest of Italian football heroes, but no relation to either one."

He smiled and removed his mirrored sunglasses. The effect was like those atom bomb tests that obliterate an entire household of mannequins.

"May I ask your name, please?" he said. "As I say, I am Giancarlo."

I should emphasize here that I am entirely heterosexual with an unblemished record of heterosexual activity of an entirely normal and honorable variety. Nevertheless, I am prepared to admit that I am affected by great-looking people — men and women. I'll assert that everyone is so affected. Suddenly encountering a great-looking person is like a weird, close-quarters meeting with a celebrity. Or a wild animal! Say, just as an example, that Oprah or an ostrich or Ed Hochuli walked into your kitchen. It's like that, it's totally unrelated to gender, and it takes awhile to get over.

"Giancarlo here was a fashion model in Paris," Hank contributed, noting that I'd said nothing to that point.

Buonorotti half-looked at him, then returned to me. He returned his sunglasses to his face. His hooves clattered back to earth.

"Is true," he said, not unpleasantly. "It is not the first thing I prefer to tell people, but, yes, I did the modeling."

"Shirtless modeling. Underwear, Swimwear," Hank added, with a peculiar, perhaps disapproving arch of his buzzcut. "One of the golf cart girls recognized him from some kinda calendar in the caddyshack ladies' room."

Buonorotti said precisely nothing. The gorgeous summer sky floated through his sunglasses. It was only then that I noticed a few actual golf cart girls, standing mute and still just a few paces away, staring at him.

"Forgive me. Very nice to meet you, Giancarlo," I said, coming to my senses and shaking his hand. "My name's U.S. Owens."

"It is my pleasure to meet you, U.S. Owens."

"Please, call me 'Ooze,'" I said, looking at Hank. "Can he wear a t-shirt and jeans on the course?"

"No," Hank boomed.

"I will find suitable attire, Oose," Buonorotti said, considering himself.

"So I need three things, Buonorotti. The first, someone who can read greens. Can you read greens? Because I can't. I'm a terrible greens-reader."

"I can," he answered. "I might say, even, that I have a gift for greens-reading."

"Great. The next thing I need is for you not to gamble on my bag. In any fashion. Dudes are gonna be gambling up and down the leaderboard, as I'm hoping you know. But not me. And not you. Are you a gambler, Buonorotti?"

"I have gambled, yes. I will not gamble on you or us. I give you my word."

"Great. So the third thing is that there's this huge, psychopathic husband after me. As it turns out, that helps me play really well. We barely know one another, so please do scan for husbands, as I would expect any pro looper to do. However, if Burr does attack me, I must insist that you stand back. I'll take care of everything."

I'd debated the ethics of involving him in the entire Burr situation, then decided it was basically unfair. Burr would come storming after me eventually, and I barely knew Buonorotti. How could I ask for his help? And he was too good-looking to be of much help anyway, in all likelihood. People with great hair are usually unreliable in a crisis.

"Are you sure, Oose?" he said. "We do have the dangerous husbands in Italy, too."

"I don't doubt it, Buonorotti."

"And I have certain skills."

"Thank you for the offer," I said. "I got it covered, Buonorotti."

I drew out my brand new, double-barreled Taser X2 stun gun from my pocket. I held it out for him. Buonorotti looked at it, then at me.

"May I ask, Oose, how big is this psychotic husband?"

"Big. 6'7". 250. Why?"

"Is that your only stun gun, Oose?"

"This is the Taser X2. It's got two shots. They say you can take down a bear with it!"

"What kind of bear?"

"Never mind, Buonorotti. An American bear. Not a tiny European bear."

"Very good, Oose."

"Don't worry, I've shot dozens of husbands with these things."

"I am quite reassured."

"You read the greens and occasionally scan for husbands. I'll do the golf and tasering."

"An excellent plan, Oose. If you will both excuse me, I will acquire an appropriate set of clothes."

Hank and I watched him depart.

"You should let Bugliotti take a few blows from this 6'7" husband," Hank advised. "I mean, he is your caddy."

"Ah, it didn't seem sporting."

"I see. Well, if he can read greens better than Harry O'Brien," Hank contributed. "I'd say you hit the jackpot, Owens!"

I'd been thinking the same thing.

I spent the next half hour casually crushing drives and caressing irons on the practice tee. It was so clear I'd be at my very peak that I stopped early, rather than over do it. It's significant to note that I hadn't a fear in the world.

As I approached the first tee for my 7:45 start, Buonorotti was ready and waiting. He wore a tidy Sennetts Harbor Club shirt, white slacks, and white sneakers.

I saw they'd paired me with a couple of millennial punks, names I recognized as up-and-comers. Foster somebody and Chick Flake. Golf names. Tight clothes. Shaved eyebrows.

"Who's this?" Chick said, as we climbed up to the tee box.

"This is Buonorotti," I said. "He's my caddy."

"Good morning, gentlemen," Buonorotti said.

Something flickered in Chick's eyes. He looked at Foster.

"You're blowing money on a caddy?" Chick continued, taking Buonorotti's hand without looking at him.

"Wait a minute," Foster said. "You don't have a husband after you, do you, Owens?"

"Don't worry about it, Potsie. You two manscapers will be fine. This husband just wants me, and I got it covered."

At that moment, the starter announced our threesome. He read out our names, just like a Major tournament. Mine was first.

I don't have a lot of money, but I spend some of it on custom Pro V1s. I have my name and a few patriotic emblems painted on them. I always start a round with a Screaming Eagle. I don't believe in much. But I believe in freaking America.

I climbed the little rise and teed up Screaming Eagle. I'd tell you I took a few practice swings, just to make this more believable, but I didn't. I just smashed it, with my easy, filthy, superwide swang.

I recall standing there, watching it, posed and torqued up like Mercury. I remember the beginnings of a prideful tear in my eye, which I somehow overcame.

"Carried a bit further than I expected," I said, knitting my brow in surprise.

Buonorotti stood over my bag, giving me the slightest of complimentary nods.

Chick and Foster each contributed a pedestrian drive, followed by a feeble approach. Only then did I arrive at my ball. It sat perky and neat in the center of the fairway. Birdsong and tumbling surf filled the air.

As I inspected my clubhead, I knew with a certainty few ever enjoy that I would swing beautifully, that I would send a gentle chip into the air, that it would lightly dent the green, that it would bounce with a proud, easy grace — not unlike the happy trot of a Lipizzaner stallion — then roll directly toward the hole and very likely drop right in it. I had no other thought in my head but this simple, delightful one.

I eyed the green. I took up my position. I gave my pant leg a pinch-up and settled in. I swung. Above my toes, like a little ticker-tape parade, blades of colonial bentgrass tumbled through the air. I watched Screaming Eagle drop and roll perhaps a dozen feet from the cup.

Eventually, after much sturm und drang, we were on the green, and it was my turn to putt.

"Buonorotti," I said. "So here's where it gets weird. I just can't putt. I got, what, 15 feet? With a couple breaks?"

An eyebrow lifted high above his right mirrored lens.

"Is that not right?"

"If you would, Oose, show me the line you think you should take."

I shrugged and did so. I knew I was way off. Nevertheless, Buonorotti's reaction was alarming.

"Please do not joke, Oose."

"I'm not joking."

He looked at me steadily. He looked at the line. He seemed to want to say something.

"This line you indicate …" he began, then stopped, the thought drifting away.

"I just need you to show me a line, Buonorotti."

"You can make shots like that drive and that wedge, but you can't putt?" Foster asked.

"Not now, Ralph Malph."

"That's right," Chick said. "That's the book on him. I remember now. With a husband after him, he can't putt."

"I don't believe it," Foster said, looking at everybody in turn. "We've all got husbands after us! It helps him?"

Buonorotti had started a wide circle around the hole. He took two measured paces in a northeasterly direction, more or less. He took a marker in his pocket. He squatted, pushed the marker into the earth, stood, and faced me.

"If you would, Oose, hit it here."

"Ha!" Chick said. "What the hell kind of line is that?"

"Hit it there?" I asked.

"He's gonna send you into the next tee box, Owens," Chick observed with satisfaction.

"I don't know, Buonorotti. The hole's in a whole other direction."

"Please, Oose. It is a practice round."

I felt my shoulders around my ears and realized I was coiled up with tension. I forced them down. I took a deep breath.

"Alright," I said.

I sidled up to the putt. I found the marker in the distance. I took a practice swing.

"Exactly half that swing, please," Buonorotti said.

I looked up at him. He'd taken off his glasses, and it had the effect of instantly obliterating every nerve or note of anxiety I felt.

I refocused on the putt.

Chick said a derisive "Good luck," but I barely noticed.

I putted, and the ball was rolling, moving unerringly toward the marker, then, in a shock, banking hard and right on a bump I never even saw.

"What the f!" Chick said, but he didn't say just "f" as the Screaming Eagle accelerated downhill now, following a tightening arc.

"It's too fast!" I cried.

"I don't think so, Oose."

Then BAM it hit the hole, bounced straight up maybe a foot and a half, dropped straight down, and rattled triumphantly in.

"Mother-of-pearl oysters!" I cheered (one of my generally unsatisfying ersatz curses).

"A brilliant putt, Oose," he countered.

"You're not wrong, Buonorotti!" I said, adding an irrepressible, if pedestrian, boo-yah!.

"What the F!!" Chick said again, with complete outrage.

"Where was that line?" Foster begged, tracing the green, hunched over, sniffing even.

"Can you do that again, Buonorotti?"

"Often I can, Oose, yes."

He took my putter.

"Wow, that's great!" was all I could manage in response.

Indeed, I had no need for further demonstrations of just how fine and, frankly, otherworldly Buonorotti was on the greens. Still, he provided them. On the second hole, he found a line that sent my putt teetering down a ridgeline, banking right and curling into the cup. On three I sank a thirty footer that changed direction five times. I never saw the hole; I just followed Buonorotti's marker! On four, he bounced my putt off a pinecone, reshaped its direction using the curve of the first cut and dropped it in.

Meanwhile, my woods and iron play only got better, goosed as I was by our incredible putting. I took four birdies and an eagle before I'd even made the turn.

Naturally, Chick and Foster unraveled. Foster, a professional golfer, topped a drive on eight that barely made it past the ladies tee. On nine, Chick plowed his ball right into the middle of a refreshment cart, bringing it (the ball, not the refreshment cart) back at us nose-high.

It all came to a head after I cranked a 380-yard power fade at 11. I was inspecting my lie, the others having finally shanked their way up to me.

"What are you going to do now?" Chick said, suddenly at my elbow.

"Approach wedge, please, Buonorotti."

"What are you going to do, Owens?"

"I'm gonna zing it back, Chick," I said, wondering why I was explaining myself.

Foster had joined Chick, right next to us. Chick was staring at me and showing a couple front teeth. Foster was staring, too, but more like one of those prairie dogs you see on TV, sort of alarmed, upright and blinky.

"You're gonna zing it in from the back?" Foster said.

"Yeah," I said.

"On this hole?"

"Yes," I said. Of course, I knew where they were going.

"Have you checked the coursebook?!" Chick said. "It'll fly right off!"

"Not today."

"This joint is stimping at like 13, Ooze!" Foster said.

"Watch this, nerds," I said, then pressed the butt of the wedge into Chick's gut, pushing him back.

With a final look at the flag, which lifted and died on a breeze, I took the wedge back easy and cut it high. It made a pleasant zip, even as a perfect, dollar-sized divot somersaulted through the air. I looked up, finding my ball exactly where she should be, arcing through the clouds.

We all heard the ball plop down. I was already handing the wedge back to Buonorotti when we heard it clang off the stick.

"Holy cow!" Chick said again.

"It didn't go in," Foster said. "I don't believe it."

"It went in," Buonorotti said, though none of us could see it.

"How do you know?" Foster said.

"I know these things," Buonorotti answered, wiping the wedge down. He looked at all of us in turn. "It was a very good shot, such as I have rarely seen."

"Thank you, Buonorotti."

"Prego."

"A good shot?" Chick said, getting emotional and even a little angry. "That shot? There are maybe a dozen guys in the world who could make that shot. On a good day! When your stimp is a seven or something!"

"A dozen?" I asked.

"Maybe two or three," Foster said.

"Maybe Tiger," Buonorotti said. "In 2002."

"Goddammit!!" Chick erupted.

"It's a matter of debate or speculation, I suppose," I said.

For a moment, I was lost in reflection at my outrageous luck. I mean, Buonorotti's shamanic greens guidance throttled up my game like a tank of nitrous oxide. He knew it. I knew it. I was standing there thinking I'd shoot in the 50s for four days straight!

So you can imagine, I hope, that I didn't put two and two together right away when I saw a figure emerge from the trees and heard Foster make the standard Husband Warning call.

"HUSBAND!" Foster cried. "HUSBAND!!!!"

"I'm gonna kill you, Owens!" was the next thing I heard. Circumstances became instantly clear. I recognized the figure storming towards me as none other than Auchincloss Hastings Burr, like a berserker in madras shorts.

Now, at this and all higher levels of golf, the always-shouted Husband Warning or "HW" is a broadly understood general alarm. Corey Pavin famously saved Fred Funk's life with an HW at Medina in '92. Likewise in '86, Craig Statler rescued Larry Mize. The HW is such a standard that even the LPGA and Asian leagues use it, in English and regardless of player orientation.

Foster made his HW with urgency, but also a certain professionalism, not unlike a lifeguard spotting a shark. This reset my focus considerably, and fear climbed my legs like little, speedy snakes. I ran in place briefly before hopping right, just in time for Burr, or more precisely, his fist and brass knuckles, to blaze past my nose.

"I'm going to kill you, Owens!!" Burr cried again, and it was very much a war cry, complete with wild eyes and a weapon, the brass knuckles, brandished above his head.

He gave chase, and we were reduced to several undignified laps around the pin. Apparently Burr didn't play the game, because he gave no thought whatsoever to pulling said pin. This was a significant break as it gave me time to wrestle the Taser X2 from my pants.

"May I be of some assistance with this husband, Oose?" I heard Buonorotti say from somewhere.

"No! Stand back, Buonorotti! Save yourself!" I answered, doing another lap around the pin.

I'd like to note here that Chick and Foster were, at best, too shocked and, at worst, too dumb, to move very far away. I mean, aiming the X2 at Burr as I ran around the pin, I nearly tripped over them a couple times. Things got a bit jumbled and dizzy. I found myself adrift in the fog of war, as I've heard it called. So much so that when I did finally fire the X2, Burr swung out of my sites at the last second and Chick swung in. Which is to say that I missed Burr and tasered Chick, who subsequently rose up on one foot, did this kind of truncated scissor kick, and collapsed.

"Ha!" Burr barked triumphantly.

I fired again, but Burr had already adapted to the asymmetry of our battlefield, seizing Foster and blocking both electrodes with Foster's neck. Foster briefly extended his tongue, did a kind of jazz-hands thing, and fell on top of Chick.

"Looks like it's just you and me now, Owens! Ha ha ha!"

It was at that precise moment that I stepped on a stray wedge. It flipped up and whacked my leg. I cried out in pain.

"HA!" Burr cheered, but I was learning and adapting, too. I instantly thought of Harry's guidance re Burr's knees and a two iron.

I took up the wedge, reversed it, pulled it back like a club.

"Good luck with that, Owens!" Burr said and took another mighty swipe with his brass knuckles.

We squared off, circling slowly. I waggled my wedge. He rolled his fists.

Burr clearly thought I intended to swing at his head. He held his arms higher, and brought his head low. It was, for me, the work of an instant to suggest such a high blow, then whack him hard, right in the side of his left knee. It folded up like a dented hat, and Burr went down in a yowl of pain.

A couple of tournament wardens came running out of nowhere, open sport jackets sailing on the wind, full bellies leading the way. Then some real police rolled in. There was a brief pigpile. Finally, they wrapped him up.

"Jiminy Freaking Christmas, Burr! I said not to attack me until Sunday, didn't I?"

"I didn't want to wait!"

"And what's with the brass knuckles?!"

"I wanted the satisfaction of smashing your face in, Owens, but without actually killing you!"

This made sense, which I had to concede.

"But didn't I tell you to bet on me, too? Didn't I tell you you would have made a fortune!?"

"I already have a fortune! Good luck winning this crappy tournament now, Owens!" he sneered, as they cuffed him. "You've got nothing to fear! Nothing at all! Ha! Ha! Ha! Ouch!"

They'd lifted him to a horizontal position and, like a rolled up carpet, hauled him off stage left.

To that point, I'd been feeling a bit grand. Only then did I realize the significance of his words. I had nothing to fear — my game, therefore, was doomed!

"You handled yourself admirably, Oose," I heard Buonorotti say. "Only rarely have I seen husbands so deranged."

"I blew it, Buonorotti!"

"How do you mean, Oose?"

Before I could answer, tournament wardens ushered me to the next tee. They clearly felt the round must continue immediately, and they were probably right. Buonorotti, meanwhile, was pulled aside for questioning.

Humming like a tuning fork, I teed a ball, swung, and did, in fact, make contact. It went long and wide, landing somewhere at sea.

I took a seven on that hole. It was a par four.

I took five more sevens. On the green at 18, I putted in for a final seven, adding up to a round of 83 and eliciting from somewhere deep inside me a cataclysm of emotion. Raising two trembling fists to the heavens, I gave a mighty howl.

"GRRELLEAHHHH!!!!!!"

"Are you okay, Oose?" Buonorotti asked, joining me only now.

I didn't answer. I'd spotted an approaching golf cart. Like Stallone in First Blood, I watched it close, setting and resetting my feet until it rolled just within arm's reach. I grabbed the kid behind the wheel and launched him into a pond. The cart whimpered to a stall. I jumped in, floored it, and gunned it for the Sennetts Harbor Club bar.

I was alone, and gratefully so, for the better part of three hours before Buonorotti materialized beside me.

"Oose," he said, with an extra few curlicues (though that may have been the booze). "May I join you?"

I flared a nostril at a neighboring stool. He took a seat.

Nothing was said for perhaps five minutes. Buonorotti folded his arms on his chest and sighed once or twice.

"I must say to you," he eventually began. "That I think, together, we were truly as good as anyone in the world — "

" — what are you doing here, Buonorotti? I mean, really?" I interrupted. I had had some time to think. "I mean, I may be crazy, but caddying European swimsuit models who are perhaps the greatest greens-readers in the game are sort of a rarity. Right? In these parts? In freaking Maine? On a freaking island? HA! HahaHAhahaha (extended cough, recovery)! Enough of a rarity certainly that one requires a freaking explanation!"

"You are right," he said. "It may be hard to believe, Oose, but I am quite wealthy. As such, I can travel the world. I have this gift for reading the greens, and so I walk the golf courses of the world in the brilliant sunlight of many brilliant days."

"Uh huh!"

"I have led a … complicated life. This walkabout, if you will, is a kind of penance. I carry other men's bags. I toil through the most beautiful of days and places. As a punishment for my many sins."

"Which are?"

"I'd rather not go into them at this moment, Oose."

"How'd you make your money?"

"Again, I'd rather not say."

"I see! So, that's all almost impossible to believe, Buonorotti."

"I know," he said. "Incidentally, I should tell you, I did post bail for Mr. Burr to get out of the prison. Alas, he needs significant treatment before he can threaten you again."

"Squirrel Nuts!"

"Do you have other questions for me?"

"If you're gonna answer like that, no."

"May I ask you a question, Oose?"

"Sure!"

"You do not gamble or swear?"

"That's right."

"Why, if I may ask?"

"For the game, Buonorotti."

"A superstition, then."

"That's right. I don't gamble. I don't swear. I am also," and here I looked around, then whispered. "I'm also celibate."

I saw his eyebrows lift above his glasses.

"That's right. Also for the game. I play better."

"These are great sacrifices."

"I know it!"

"Particularly the celibacy, Oose."

"You're telling me, Buonorotti!"

I downed what remained of my current drink, then signaled for another.

"So the violent men who stalk and terrify you are the primary secret to your success," Buonorotti said, almost to himself. "Together with no gambling, no swearing and no bada-bing. When did you first discover this, Oose?"

"At Congressional. In the US Open in 2011."

He said nothing.

"Yeah! I was on the PGA Tour!" I said, looping a finger in the air. "Google it."

"And you were playing like this because someone was trying to kill you then?"

"Yes, as a matter of fact. My ex-wife. The first one. I have three ex-wives. Each one more dangerous than the next!"

"Tell me what happened, please," Buonorotti said.

"I got my card that year. I finished in the top 10 at Q School. I played my first PGA Tour event in New Mexico. I finished fifth. Won more money than I'd ever seen in my life. Meanwhile, the first ex-wife was cheating on me. Naturally, being a woman, she convinced herself it was also my fault. It's a long story having to do with the fact that I long suspected she was cheating on me, and accordingly I couldn't, you know, do it anymore with her."

"Do what?"

"The bada-bing."

"Ah."

"She thought that that meant I was in fact cheating on her. She thought I was all used up by some other chick. She didn't believe the story I invented that I was celibate to keep my focus on golf. So, she walked out on me, but BUT she was still so angry she kept following me, going to all the tournaments, all the events, all the practice rounds. Every now and then, she'd come tearing out of the gallery and attack me. That only made me play better, which enraged her more because she thought I dumped her so I could earn all this money with the other chick. Who didn't exist!"

"Yes. I see. Women are a mystery we cannot solve."

"Right, well, so she got angrier and angrier, and I just kept playing better and better. Pretty soon, as I said, I had my PGA Tour card. The next thing you know, I've got a couple top-five finishes. Next thing after that, I'm playing in the US Open at Congressional, and I'm paired with freaking Wink Paddington on Sunday. And I'm in the hunt!"

"My goodness!"

I snorted.

"And I'm tearing it up," I said. "Now, Buonorotti, do you know anything about golf gambling?"

"A bit. Not much. Little. Very little. Continue."

"Well, in any tournament, there's action all up and down the board. These guys, if they don't think they're gonna win it, they keep it interesting by betting on every little thing. Five hundred bucks says you put your drive in the woods. A grand says I can smash that BMW's windshield. Worst score pays the best score $10,000. That sort of thing. And me? As this newcomer who's on a tear? I'm the center of the biggest action. And the biggest high roller of them all? Wink Paddington. The California Kid. The OC OG. He carries half a million dollars in his freaking golf bag. He's got like $250k on some kind of spread between us, and he's watching me like a hawk! Sure, he still wore that big goofy grin, but every time I turn around, there he is. 'Hey, buddy!' he'd say. Every time. Or he'd wink! Ever had a celebrity wink at you -"

"- Yes, I have -"

"It's terrifying! Especially when is name is 'Wink'!"

"I do not doubt it, Oose."

"And me, all I can think about is that she's out there. Somewhere. And there's no way in heck she'll let me win this thing. She's probably in a tree with a sniper rifle and a bunch of sawgrass stuck in her hair. The entire effect is like the world's greatest performance enhancing drug. I'm smashing 350 yard drives, draining birdie putts, drawing and fading and stinging and zinging balls all over the place. Burt Stiltz, my old caddy, is guiding me like a blind man through every putt. The crowd's going wild. Wink Paddington is right there at each shot, like he's my best friend, saying 'Hey, buddy!' and 'You're doing super!' and 'Boo-yah!,' all with that crazy smile! He's even fist pumping and fist bumping me through all by best shots. All of sudden I'm on the back nine. I'm coming in, but all I can think is, I'm a dead man! And that's when it happens …"

I paused. I stared at nothing. I could see that afternoon like it was yesterday.

"What happens, Oose?"

"… we're standing there. Giess Freaking VanMikels is teeing off. He's our third. The cameras, for just the briefest of moments, are on VanMikels. That's when Paddington leans over to me. He takes off his hat …"

I paused here, again. Just like it was this very morning, I could see Paddington's pink, untanned forehead, his super-tanned face, his big eyes, all leaning right into me.

"What does he say, Oose?"

"He whispers 'Hey, buddy! I took care of that thing for ya.'"

"What thing did he take care of, Oose?"

"He found my ex!" I continued. "He had her hauled off! I'm staring at him. He's wearing that 'Howdy, neighbor!' smile of his. Like he's done me this huge favor! Like he has no idea what's going on! But I'm here to tell you right now, Wink Paddington knows what's going on all the time, everywhere. Like J. Edgar Hoover. Or Stalin! 'My security guys,' he says. 'They took care of that thing.' That's what he said. *That thing*. He'd figured it out! He realized that the root of my play was my crazy ex-wife. I didn't even understand it, but Wink Paddington did!"

"How, Oose?"

"My caddy told him!"

"Not your caddy!"

"Burt Stiltz! My caddy!"

"And then what?"

"So VanMikels smashes his drive, and I come back to life. 'You're home free, Gus,' Paddington whispers. He thought my name was Gus for some reason. I forgot about that. He called me Gus all day long! 'Go rip the cover off it, Gus!' he says. But he didn't mean it. He had that crazy Californian twinkle in his eye. What he really meant was, 'You're a dead man, Owens. I figured you out. I'm gonna win this tournament, and you're gonna lose because I figured you out, punk. I'm Wink Freaking Paddington!'"

"Are you sure that's what he meant, Oose?"

"Yeah!"

"Paddington always seemed like the very best public figure and sportsman. Despite the tight shirts and left-handedness."

"Well, he's not!"

"And you might even say, Oose, that Wink Paddington saved your life in this story."

"How do you figure?!"

"Hmm. And then what happened?"

"I fell apart. I took three consecutive triple bogies. He won $250,000 off me. Even though he lost the tournament, he looked and behaved like he won it! So did everyone else!"

"I see. And what happened to you?"

"With nothing and no one to terrorize me, I was off the tour at the end of the year! Living out of my car, eating Grape Nuts three meals a day and doing this crummy PI work to stay alive!"

Buonorotti sat back in his chair. For a long time, or at least until I finished my nacho plate, he stared into space. I was eating through most of this conversation, I regret to add.

"Oose, I'll ask an indelicate question, if I may: would you permit me to threaten you?"

"You?"

"Yes," Buonorotti frowned and nodded. "I am in fact a very dangerous man. I have killed … how many is a dozen?"

"12."

"I have killed a dozen men."

"While underwear modeling?"

"Before," he said. "I was in the Foreign Legion. And the Cosa Nostra."

"Really?"

"Is entirely true. Oh, and I killed a couple other people while I was in jail."

"Jail?"

"Yes. Devil's Island. Very bad."

"Huh," I said. I looked him over again. "Ah, you couldn't do it, Buonorotti."

"What? I couldn't kill you right now?"

"No, you couldn't. Or even if you could and did, I'd never believe it until it actually happened."

"Why, Oose?"

"Because," I said, pointing a nacho. "My instincts tell me that you're fundamentally a decent person."

He seemed surprised by this, so I continued.

"I mean, you put up with me for 18 holes, then you bailed out Burr, then you showed up here."

"Well, Oose, you owe me money for the caddying."

"Buonorotti, if I gave you money right now, I am absolutely certain wouldn't take it."

"Give it to me, then."

"I don't have any."

"I'll kill you."

"No, you won't."

"With my bare hands I will do so."

"Alright," I craned my neck. "Here! Strangle me!"

"It would be better to kill you quietly outside."

"Much better! Let's go!"

I got up. Buonorotti remained.

"C'mon!" I said. "I'm shafting you!"

I tugged at him. Nothing.

"See," I said. "I knew it. It's these keen PI instincts. Another cruel, useless gift of fate!"

I took my seat. Buonorotti seemed almost helpless.

"I *was* a criminal. I *killed* many people. Do you not believe me?"

"I'm sure it was all entirely justifiable."

"I am humbled, Oose."

"We played like gods today, Buonorotti," I said. "Maybe that's all it is. I can tell that means something to you."

"Indeed we did, and it does."

We stared at the Golf Channel for another half hour. He stood.

"It was an honor to meet you, Oose Owens. I am afraid I must return to my journey now."

"Give me your phone number. I'll call you as soon as I scare up the next husband. We'll be gods again!"

"I don't have a mobile phone. It is a tool of the devil."

"Of course you don't."

We shook hands.

"Via con dios, my friend," he said.

It may have been the booze, but he more or less vanished at that point.

I remained at the bar for an untold number of hours. On the television, the various millennial nobs who now dominate the tour were smacking pedestrian drives and boorish irons all over the place, as if to mock me. In a way, they succeeded: my mind eventually turned to my grim need for actual money. I need two to three PI gigs a month to stay in the black. Owing to my obsession with this specific tournament, I had started the month with, approximately and under very general rules of accounting, zero PI gigs. Zero underway. Zero lined up. Zero. I marked time with a couple more drinks I couldn't afford.

The afternoon slipped away. I remember cackling children and clinking silverware. I remember the sun setting and a jeweled glow that filled the room. The clock on the wall ticked towards 9:00 pm. Thus, it was against the background of a beautiful, lingering summer evening that my next gig announced itself.

"Hi," it said. "Mr. Owens?"

I turned and, for a moment, was redirected toward the floor, which seemed to rise up as if to embrace me. It was okay though. I stabilized. I completed my turn and slid back into a corner of my stool.

I faced a young woman, beaming, a short swirl of blonde hair, boobs pushing around a polo top, a blink-and-you-miss-it tennis skirt, and long, tan legs that ended in bright, white sneakers. Girlish, eager, rich. Club tart would be the obvious read. Of course, as a pro athlete, I expect women like this everywhere.

"Good evening," I said, which came out with a certain Hitchcock rhythm I occasionally acquire when over-served.

"You're U.S. Owens! The golfer who does private eye work?"

"I am."

She took a seat next to me.

"My name is Jiggly Jones!" she said, like a cheer.

"... *Jiggly* Jones?"

"I know," she rolled her eyes. "My real name is Georgia Jones, but I've always been sort of jiggly, so friends started calling me that! Anyway, I think my husband's on our boat with another woman. I just saw you here, Mr. Owens, and thought, you could go check."

"... What? Right now?"

She sat even straighter and nodded.

"Yes. Please. Right now."

"Well, Jiggly, in full disclosure," I just couldn't shake this Hitchcock thing (dis-clo-o-zure). "I've been drinking."

"I can drive you!"

"Actually, I'm completely tanked."

"You just need to look at the boat!"

"And I've got to go to bed early. I have an early tee time, and it's the first round of the tournament."

"I'll pay you $500/hr!"

This stopped me momentarily. I charge $100/hr.

"What's your husband's name?"

"Bowdoin Jones."

"Your husband's name is Bowdoin."

"That's right. Like the college."

"College?"

"There's a college here in Maine named Bowdoin."

"Do they own it?"

"Probably!"

"Is your husband dangerous at all?"

"No! Not my Bowdoin!"

I blinked a bit at the suddenness of it all. I pushed my fingers through my hair.

"Please, Mr. Owens. You're the only thing that could," and here her chin and lower lip started to quiver. "... that could hold our marriage together!"

With that she started crying like a riveting machine. I found some bar napkins and gave them to her. Instead, she took my hand along with the napkins and pulled it into her chest. Where her boobs were! I looked around. Every eye was on us!

When she finally let my hand go, I immediately used it to wave over the bartender. Jiggly declined a drink. Mine arrived in the next moment, and I downed it in a gulp.

"Jiggly ..." I said, turning back to her.

"I'll give you $600/hr," she said. "I'll pay you for two hours right now!"

She produced $1,200 in cash from her purse.

I thought for a moment, nodded, then said, "Alright."

"Thank you!" she cheered. "My car's outside!"

Then she left a kiss on my cheek so delicate I can still feel it today.

The kiss had a powerful, sobering effect, as I have noticed women's kisses often do. It would probably be too much to say that I was actually, instantly, entirely sober, but I felt entirely sober, and that's really half the battle.

The next thing I knew, we were in her little car and careening through the pines. For my own digestive stability, I kept a tight focus on a blade of moonlight that clung to the hood.

Eventually, we slowed, took a turn, and descended into a parking lot. Below us, nestled among a few piney mountains, was little Sennetts Harbor itself.

"Kill the lights," I said to Jiggly, not a little like a driving instructor.

"Great!" she answered and did so.

"And park over here, away from everyone," I added, and she did that, too.

There seemed to be the same arrangement of lobster boats, sailboats and *look-at-me-world!* boats in the harbor. Lights twinkled here and there. The faint jingle of cocktail activity traveled to us from a few different sources. For the most part, however, night had settled in and everything was dark, moonlit and serene.

"Which boat is it?" I asked.

"The big, white one."

"They're all big and white."

"It's the biggest one."

"What's its name?"

"The Flustered Lush," she said. "It says 'Flustered Lush' right there on the back. In black and gold letters. You can read it a mile away!"

"You stay here," I said and was about to tilt out of the car when her hand fell on mine. My hand, let it be noted, was on my thigh.

"Be careful!" she said in a hush.

There was a huskiness in her tone — like Raquel Welch huskiness — that made me look back up. As a normal man sitting in a car in the distant corner of a parking lot with a beautiful girl on a moonlit night (and her hand on my thigh), I hesitated to leave. I knew she was playing me. Women are able to do that sort of thing, even when they don't actually or deliberately intend to do so.

My hesitation lasted only a moment. I do have three ex-wives. I extracted my hand and rolled out. Golf is a game that requires a certain lightness of spirit, and for today's round I'd worn a shirt that was a kind of tangerine color with a little bit of shimmer. I had matching pants. And white shoes. All of which is to say that, visually, I was somewhat compromised for surveillance work. As such, I stuck to the shadows while descending to the pier, and I remained therein (the shadows, that is) as I scanned the harbor with my binoculars (I'd grabbed them from the Fury before hopping in Jiggly's car). I started tracking left to right, though it all got a bit tricky as the tide turned the boats, concealing more than a handful of their names, emblazoned as they usually are on the stern. Not to mention the general, queasy, surfy way my vision was swimming around. Eventually I found the boat, though. "The Flustered Lush" was etched in big black letters with a gold outline. A pump expelled a steady stream of water from just below the "t." I lifted my binoculars to the deck as the boat turned. It was close to 40' long, perhaps 20' across the beam. A cabin sat in the middle with three windows, all dark.

I watched a bit longer, but nothing happened. I lowered the binoculars. It was only then that I noticed that no dingy or launch floated behind The Flustered Lush, unlike its various boat neighbors. My mind was too hazy to put two and two together, but you know how these things go. You see something, and something about that something says 'Man, there's something wrong with this picture?' You often encounter this in horror movies, where a beautiful young girl returns to the car or bedroom or shed where she'd been necking with the captain of the football team. He's gone, usually in a permanent sense, but she thinks he's still around. "'Billy?' she calls. 'Come on out, Billy. I'm horny again!'" Not hearing a response, she's briefly puzzled. Then, out of focus, our masked killer emerges, a huge item of lawn equipment in his hands. Often, for pathos, he's wearing Billy's underwear.

Well, effectively, that's what happened here. Said figure rose up behind me (sans mask and underwear) and announced himself.

"What the hell are you looking at?" it said. "Are you looking for Jiggly Jones? Well! You're not going to find her here, pal!"

I spun around. I think it speaks to my startled state of mind that I asked the next couple questions.

"Who are you?!"

"My name is Bowdoin Jones!"

"Like the college?"

He didn't answer, as he found himself entangled with a garden hose while trying to emerge from the bushes. No matter. He cursed a bit, took half the hose with him and came for me.

He was enormous, as Jiggly Jones had implied, with a college-noseguard-gone-to-seed girth and power. Discretion being the better part of valor, I ran. It turned out, there was nowhere to go, really, unless I wanted to swim for it. He'd boxed me up against the harbor, and, as such, we were reduced to a little chicken chase within the confines of the pier.

"What are you doing?" I cried over my shoulder, as I ran and dodged. "Stop it!"

"Stay away from my wife!"

"Buddy, I just met your wife!"

"Sure, you did, Owens!"

"She approached me!"

"Ha!"

"She hired me! I'm a private eye! She thought you were cheating on her!"

"Lies!"

"No! Truths!!!"

"It's all over!"

"What's all over?!"

"Your affair with Jiggly!"

"My affair with Jiggly?"

"That's right!"

"Wait! You called me 'Owens'!" I said. "How do you know my name?!"

But by this point he'd closed enough distance that he didn't feel the need to respond.

He took two steps and grazed my ear with a full karate kick. I'm pretty sure he also said, "Hiyahh!"

I reacted instinctively. A couple dozen generations of war-fighting DNA bubbled up — DNA I thought had entirely passed me by — and I hit him. Squarely. Just below his right eye.

You would think that that part of Bowdoin Jones's face might be boney, and in fact it was. Quite boney. Boney like a rock, and for a moment I was certain I'd shattered my hand and, of course, my golf game for the next several months.

"Zippity-Do-Da!" I yelped, cradling by hand as if it were a wounded bird.

Bowdoin, for his part, didn't physically react to the blow at all. It seemed to bounce off him. Vocally, however, he cried out, then dropped to his knees. It was so much drama that my pain seemed to evaporate. I mean, he crumpled up in a ball. His face went through multiple, Brando-esque states of high expression: agony, grief, reaction to a bad smell, rapture, idiocy, and, finally, indignation.

"You're a dangerous psychopath, Owens!" he howled.

"You started it!" I countered.

Bowdoin contributed nothing further, but abruptly got up, then scrambled away, leading with his left-side and hobbling like a wounded gorilla. He dropped into a launch, the launch itself dropped a couple fathoms into the water, and he yanked back the cord to start the motor. It buzzed to life. He threw off a line and opened the throttle.

"Stop stalking my wife!" Bowdoin cried as he pushed out into the darkness. "My wife, Jiggly Jones!!"

"What are you talking about?!" I called back, listening to the echoes.

My hand ached. My lungs burned. Figures now emerged from other boats, eager to see what the tumult had been about. I decided it was time to leave and high-tailed it back up to an empty parking lot.

"Jiggly?" I called.

Jiggly and her sporty little car had vanished.

CHAPTER THREE — THURSDAY

Staggering drifter-like along the shoulder of the road, I somehow found the hotel. Bewildered, exhausted, and increasingly, ruinously sober, I tripped into my bed, thought briefly about pulling off my golf spikes, and went out like a light.

I awoke to a double-ear-clap boom, a burst of violet light, and a kind of multidimensional, all-consuming rattle. I noticed as well that the various little things in the room — toothbrushes, frames, lamps, remote controls — seemed to bounce and vibrate around. Then, just as suddenly, all went perfectly still.

I understood these events initially as the obvious and deserved result of a long night. Soon thereafter, as if to confirm these scoundrel's instincts, a massive hangover decanted itself into my senses like mustard gas.

I crawled my way to the bathroom and took a scalding hot shower. Feeling half human, I wrapped myself up into a new outfit, reattached my spikes, told myself that somehow, some way, I might break 90 this morning, and clattered down to the Fury.

I had a 9:18 start, and I wanted to get in a full breakfast beforehand. I drove again through tall pines, beneath pretty Dogwoods, past tasteful Capes and around the loop that circumnavigated Sennetts Harbor. A campfire smell rose on the breeze. In the distance, perhaps 500 yards out, a column of flame mottled the air.

A policeman redirected traffic away from the harbor and onto a detour that emerged briefly from the trees. It gave me a good look down at the entirety of the harbor, where I saw a burning boat. A meteor of fire spun round in the cabin area, presumably fed by substantial fuel tanks. The sail, as well, burned and flapped about, looking vaguely moth-eaten and rimmed with wormy embers. Ah, I thought, that sonic boom this morning wasn't a hangover, but instead an explosion associated with this burning boat. I suppose it says something about the mania with which I approach a round of golf that I speculated no further.

When stopped on a nice day in my convertible, people feel free to address me, cops especially. As I dumbly considered the boat below and waited to be waved through, a nearby cop shook his head at me.

"Boat explosion," he said, throwing a thumb over his shoulder.

"Yep," I observed.

"I wish I could blow up my boat," he added.

"Ha," I replied. "No one hurt, I hope?"

"Don't know yet," he said, then, with a signal from up ahead, sent me forward.

Again, no connections made among my various neurons and synapses, which one can only presume were firing normally, though at some kind of low and erratic wattage.

I parked the Fury, hauled my bag to the tournament tent, and went inside the club. The player's breakfast was in full swing. Young men in ridiculous outfits milled about, tittered quietly, or simply stuffed their faces. I filled my plate, then found Dirks Svensen at the far end of the buffet, clearly waiting for me. Next to yours truly, he's usually the oldest guy at the tournament. And he still looks terrific. White-blonde hair, huge forehead, a nose you could break up ice with, and a tendency to blink way too much. Rather startling in total effect.

"Have you heard, Ooze?" he said, in his singsong accent punctuated by the blinking. "About de fire in de harbor?"

"I saw the smoke."

A couple other golfers joined us, staring at me. Old-timers. Mac Griffin, Hank Henry, and English cad Cuthbert "Cocky" Brill.

"You saw de smoke?" Dirks asked.

"Yes, a boat blew up," I said. "In de harbor."

Dirks looked from me to the others, then pulled his chin in tight against his neck.

Cocky raised a hand to calm Dirks down.

"Is that weird?" I asked, forking up a sausage link from the buffet.

"Did you have anything to do with this boat explosion, Ooze?" Cocky asked, in his nasally accent. "We saw you talking to that bird at the bar last night."

"Why would I have anything to do with a boat explosion?"

"As I say, mate," Cocky continued, his left eye seeming to get bigger as he talked. "We saw you talking to that bird last night."

"That bird," I said. "Was a client. Yes, I am working a case on her behalf. What does she have to do with the boat explosion?"

"What's her name, then?"

"I can't tell you that."

"Was it Jiggly Jones?"

"Of course not," I snorted.

"That's a yes," Griffin said over his shoulder at a gathering crowd.

"Shit," Hank contributed.

"Have you not heard?" Cocky said, lifting an open-mouthed frown. "Do you know nothing about the details of the event?"

"The event being …"

"The boat explosion!" Griffin said.

"The goddamn boat explosion," Hank added.

"The boat explosion?" I asked, but I was simply being difficult now.

"Yes, man!" Cocky trilled. "The boat explosion!"

"I've heard nothing," I said with another snort of indignation. "Why don't you fellas enlighten me as to what I should know about a boat explosion and a so-called Jiggly Jones?"

It was at this moment that my mind started sputtering to life, but it did so slowly, and I paid keen attention to Hank's following remarks.

"The boat that blew up was the Flushed Lunch," Hank said. "It exploded in a massive fireball this morning, far bigger than a full tank of boat fuel would generate, or so I've been led to believe by various policemen. That boat, as I'm sure you no doubt know, belongs to one Bowdoin Jones. Married to one Georgia Jones. Also known as Jiggly Jones. Bowdoin and Jiggly Jones of Chappaqua, Fisher's Island and Palm Desert. None other than the same Jiggly Jones broad you were seen with last night ... Are you okay, Ooze?"

Somewhere in the middle of Hank's oration, it all came quickly into focus, and I choked on the sausage link. Or, I should clarify, half of it. I vaporized the other half in a cough/sneeze.

"Shit," Hank said, observing my gagging. "Owens is in it up to his eyeballs!"

The younger players had all arrived by this point. Cocky knew he was speaking for an audience now.

"They think it's bloody arson, Owens!" Cocky said, glaring, judging, his one eye getting still bigger and, if anything, googlier. "They have footage of a man wrestling with the boat owner on the pier last night!"

My mind worked in a series of flashes. It was all I could do to smother the glee surging inside me.

"Was anyone hurt?" I asked.

"That's beside the point!" Cocky said. "Owens is trouble again. He's gonna play great, dammit, and what I want to know is, what I think we're all entitled to know is — "

" — They can't find the husband, but she's fine," Hank interrupted, answering me. "Better than fine. I saw her strutting around the veranda a half hour ago."

"Like a stripper!" Griffin added.

"And they can't arrest you for murder if they don't have a body, right?" I asked.

"Who do I look like, Owens?" Hank said. "Matlock?"

"That's all beside the bloody point!" Cocky said, adding a finger jab. "What I wanna know is: Was it you, Owens?"

"I'm entirely innocent, Cocky, old man."

"But you were with that leggy blonde bird," he countered. "She had her hands practically on your bait and tackle!"

"My bait and tackoo?"

I don't like Cocky, it should be noted.

I smiled brightly at him. My mood was climbing through the sky faster than a Saturn V rocket. With my eyes still set on Cocky, I shot out a hand and swatted Hank Henry in the nuts, doubling him over. A flurry of whispers and hums filled the room.

"Anyone else going low today?" I added, scanning the crowd. "And I mean, super low? On the scoresheet, that is?"

"Were you involved in this?" Griffin now asked, at Cocky's behest.

"Did I blow up a boat in the harbor last night?" I said. "To save my golf game and mercilessly crush this tournament and everyone in it? No, I did not. I do think I was set up, however, which is just as good. Maybe better!"

"But they vill vant to question you in dis arson or possibly murder investigation, Oose!" Dirks observed.

"That's what happens when you get set up, Dirks! Who's going to come in second today, fellas?" I said to the gallery, some of whom had already descended into their phones, putting out the word and taking gambling action.

"Yeah, well, look here, mate!" Cocky declared. "You still gotta putt, innit? And no doubt you'll shag that into a cocked hat!"

And that's when I had my second revelation.

"Stick it in a rump roast!" I declared. "I gotta find Buonorotti!"

Men without phones are cagey types. At the very least, they're hard to locate when you're in a jam. Such was the case with Buonorotti. Nor did I have much time. I was booked for a 9:18 start, as mentioned, and the circumstances had not come fully into focus for me until around 8:30. As such, I spent that time flying around town in the Fury, dashing in and out of a half dozen bed and breakfasts, sprinting through restaurants, sliding down the aisles of an Independent Grocers Alliance (on my golf spikes) and only finally finding him, at precisely 8:59, sitting in an Adirondack chair on the front lawn of a place called the Asticou Inn.

I skidded to a stop and stood up in the Fury.

"What the heck are you doing, Buonorotti?"

"Hello, Oose," he said. "I am reading and drinking coffee and later I am going to the next town. There is no work here for me, I'm afraid."

"Yeah, well, there's work now. I'm a suspect in a murder investigation!"

He didn't immediately react, which was obviously understandable.

"Well, an arson-slash-missing-persons investigation at least! They set me up. I didn't do it! Isn't that terrific? I'm gonna kill it out there, Buonorotti, that's the point, no pun intended, but listen! I need you. I need you on the greens. Reading things. We gotta get back together. This is it, man! It's our shot!"

"Yes," he said, clearly now tuning in. "Yes, I see, Oose."

"So get in the freaking car!"

But he hesitated.

"What's the problem?"

"What would be the terms, Oose, if I may ask?"

"You caddy. I golf. As you know, there's no gambling on my bag. At all. Whatsoever. To compensate for that, I'll give you freaking half of anything I win. Isn't that fantastic?"

"It is very generous," he said.

"Isn't it!" I said. "And we'll just keep going. Tournament after tournament. I mean, these murder investigations can take years! I'll keep giving you half of whatever I make!"

"And no gambling."

"No freaking way, man. C'mon! Let's go, buddy!"

"I see."

Still, he didn't move.

"What?!"

"Oose, I must admit, I did have certain reservations about how we played yesterday. It wasn't appropriate to discuss them last night …"

" … What reservations?"

"There were things you said …"

"What things?!"

"Certain things, Oose, after you hit a super shot …"

"WHAT THINGS?!"

"Something like 'Mezzo Meeese ZOOOOH Ney? Mizzonney?'"

"'Me so horny'?"

"Yes, that is it. You said it after several shots. You said also, 'Is very nazz' …"

"Uh huh!"

"… and 'Woo woo woo woo.'"

"Sure! So what!"

"What do those mean, Oose?"

"'Is very nice' is from Borat. Did you see that movie?"

"No."

"'Woo woo woo woo' is a Martin Lawrence thing."

"I do not know this Martin Lawrence."

"Well, that's too bad, because he's a genius," I said. "But, hey Buonorotti, that's my brand! I'm an exciting, irreverent player! And I don't swear! These are my snarky, nineties-ish references!"

He took off his glasses now. His eyes went crazy wide.

"There is a Goddess of Golf, Oose."

"Okay?!"

"A demon goddess. These things you say, Oose. They offend her. She will make you pay for such vanity."

"Well," I guffawed. "It didn't affect our round today, did it?"

"Did it not?" he answered.

He had a point.

"Right, so you want me to shut up on the course. FINE!"

He smiled his magnificent smile.

"I can't tell you how happy that makes me, Oose."

"Great, get in the freaking car!"

"And you will do everything I say on the greens," he said, replacing his glasses. "You will follow all my shot-making directions, in fact?"

"All of it!"

"OK, Oose."

"OK, Buonorotti!"

I did perhaps 300 MPH returning to the Sennetts Harbor Club. Arriving, I fish-tailed to a stop, peppering the Port-a-Potties with gravel.

"We'll park it for real later!" I said to Buonorotti, then yanked my two iron from the backseat. "Bring the bag!"

I ran for the tee.

I was the 38th player to tee off that morning, but I had by far the biggest crowd. The word was out. I scampered hand-and-foot up the hill to the small tee box, arriving at exactly 9:18. As I caught my breath, one of the tour wardens said, "You're late and you're up, Owens" which was pretty obvious the way nothing was happening, with the tee box empty and everyone staring at me. I shoved a tee and ball into the turf, then stood back up and spun around. I'd tell you I did a waggle or even a practice swing, but I did neither. I just continued my turn, hauling back mid-spin, and crushing it. The ball hissed like an angry snake for about 75 yards and ascended into the clouds.

There was a small round of stunned applause. I pulled up my tee, flipped it to a little kid and started toward the fairway.

It would be perfect, and everybody knew it.

I played like a god through the front nine. From almost every shot, I could smell the fire of The Flustered Lush, and it served like some kind of holy PED. On the green at six, I could even hear it crackle as I drained a 30-foot putt that broke three ways. Downhill. I didn't even know where the hole was! I just did what Buonorotti told me!

I had a 27 at the turn. From the tee box on 10, I could see three policemen on the lawn by the practice green. They appeared to be the entire local force and were accompanied by three firemen. They all locked onto me as I climbed the tee box, but a squat policeman, set in the middle of all of them, commanded my attention. It was obvious he was in charge. Our eyes met, and I knew at once that he wanted to pin everything on me. My heart soared!

Said policeman kept staring, adding something like a sneer. I did an about-face, knowing I had his full attention, and blistered a 360 yard drive (carrying 320).

I birdied 10 and 11. On the tee box at 12, I discovered this policeman now in the gallery. At 15, I found him and a fireman standing over my second shot, not ten feet away.

My partner's caddy approached me, putting a hand over his cell phone and raising his chin to ask a question.

"What are you carrying on your card, Ooze?"

"I'm nine under," I answered, loud enough for the cop to hear.

"Shit," the caddy said. "Shit. Shit! I mean, Wow!"

The caddy returned to his cell. There was a brief, testy conversation, and again he covered his phone and raised his head for another question.

"How are you feeling?"

"Why?" I said, primarily to the policeman. "Are you taking bets?"

"No," the caddy answered, following my line of vision. "I'm concerned about your health."

"Is betting on golf legal in this state?"

"Betting on golf," the caddy answered. "Is illegal in every state. How are you feeling?"

"I feel like Evil Freaking Knievel when he's fifty feet in the air, knowing he's going to land a crazy-ass jump."

He relayed the message. I kept staring at the cop. He had longish, blonde, very straight hair and matching mustache — like Captain Kangaroo with a badge.

"Tell your friend," I added, addressing the caddy. "I'm going to eagle this hole."

And I did.

I birdied two more. On 16 I skipped a ball off the water and onto the green, pin high. And it was what I meant to do. On 17, I scorched another two-iron stinger 275 yards, but just ten feet off the ground. I'd told Buonorotti beforehand that I would just pop right through this hole in the trees about eight feet up. I pointed out that it was barely the size of a trash can lid. I smashed through it like a circus act.

Approaching the green at 18, I was leading by 11 and had a 56 on my card. The 18th green sits up high, and as I climbed it, the broad, cedar-shingled facade of the Sennetts Harbor Club rose in the distance. A crowd awaited. In the middle of it, standing perfectly still, was my policeman. Like the kid in The Omen!

A tournament judge joined me briefly, letting me know that I was a stroke away from the club record. He peeled off. My ball was ten feet from the hole with no break or pitch. Or so I was told. I let Buonorotti wave me in, and I drained it for the course record. A cheer boomed over the sweet, early afternoon breeze, and I touched my cap.

I staggered down from the green. The crowd met me, a small riot of cacklers and backslappers. My policeman stood beside the scoring shed.

"Mr. Owens? My name is Lieutenant Bob Lunt. Could I have a word with you?"

"Sure, Lieutenant," I answered, swallowing my glee. "What's this all about?"

"We'll talk about it in a moment. I've reserved a room in the club. My deputy will bring you there."

I turned in my card and followed the aforementioned deputy into the clubhouse, through various halls and finally into a little, windowless room. The deputy exited, shutting the door behind Buonorotti, me and Lieutenant Bob Lunt.

"Please," Lunt said. "Have a seat."

"Thank you," I said, joining him at a little table. Buonorotti took a chair in the corner.

"And you are?" the policeman asked him.

"My name is Giancarlo Scillaci Buonorotti."

"Fine," the policeman said, making a note in a spiral pad on the table. "My name, as I mentioned to Mr. Owens, is Lieutenant Bob Lunt. I'm with the Sennetts Harbor Police Department. I'm here about the boat explosion you may have noticed this morning in the harbor."

"Boat explosion?" I said.

I sat up straighter, looking extremely earnest.

"Yes," Lunt answered, studying me, then Buonorotti, and indicating a note of distaste in his cocked mustache. "A boat you may be familiar with, Mr. Owens."

"A boat I may be familiar with?"

"Can you tell me where you were last night?"

"Where I was last night?"

"Just answer the questions, please. You don't need to repeat them."

"I was here," I answered, raised my hands with a shrug, then pivoting to Buonorotti, who kept his mirrored eyes on Lunt.

"That's funny," Lunt said. "Because we have footage of someone very much like you at the pier last night."

"And I was also at the pier. As well as here. I was in both places."

"Ahh ..." Lunt said. He raised and lowered the hat on his knee. This seemed an invitation to continue.

"Alright," I said. "Alright. I can see you're a clever one, Sergeant Lunt — "

" — Lieutenant Lunt."

" — Lieutenant? Really? My compliments. Yes. I was at the pier. As you no doubt inferred," and here I gestured with both hands at my colorful sports attire. "I'm a professional golfer. I'm also, alas, not so successful that I need not do other things to make a living. The primary other thing that I do, then, is private investigative work. I can do it on my schedule, so it means I can still compete in certain pro circuits."

"Fascinating," Lunt said. "You were there on PI business?"

"That's right."

"Who's the client?"

"Well …"

I didn't continue.

"'Well' what?" Lunt said.

"I'm afraid that's a matter of PI-client privilege," I said, trying to express a certain collegial regret.

Lunt frowned.

"You want me to pretend there is such a thing as PI-client privilege?"

"There's no need to pretend. It's real."

He turned his hat on his knee.

"Mmm-hmm," Lunt said. "I can pretend you're obstructing justice, and then, you know, I can throw you both in real jail."

"I can see we're both professionals and men of the world, as are Buonorotti and me, and no doubt you, Lieutenant," I got a little turned around here, but was nevertheless feeling it, so I kept rolling. "So, in this instance and under the circumstances of this dramatic boat explosion, I'll set aside PI-client privilege as well as gentlemanly discretion for the greater cause of justice."

"Great," Lunt said. "So, you're a PI, and you were doing what all PIs do, which is sleazy divorce work. That's what you were going to say?"

I allowed myself to bristle briefly and visibly.

"I was in the employ of one Jiggly Jones."

"Georgia 'Jiggly' Jones."

"Yes, Lieutenant. How did you know?"

"Just keep telling me what you were doing for Mrs. Jones, please."

"Right," I said. "Well, Mrs. Jones thought her husband, Mr. Jones, was cheating on her. She thought he was with another woman on their boat, and she asked me to go check it out."

"I see," Lunt said. He looked at me and Buonorotti, then he reached behind his chair and pulled up a manilla folder. He produced some reading glasses and began flipping through the folder's contents.

"What's that?" I asked, barely smothering my excitement.

"This," he said, pulling up a couple big photographs, inspecting them over his glasses, then extending them to me. "This is a file the husband was keeping."

"Mr. Jones was keeping this file?"

"That's right. Mr. Bowdoin Jones."

"And what are these?" I said. "Pictures?"

I saw my condo. The Fury was parked out front. Beside it was a little, white BMW.

"This is my house!"

"Is that your car?"

"Yes!"

"Who does the white BMW belong to?"

"I don't know!" I answered. I looked at the other picture. "That car is here, too! And there's the Fury again, right next to it! Why, you'd know my car anywhere! And I believe that was the motel I stayed in for the Winchester tournament!"

"Uh-huh," Lunt said.

"Who's BMW is that, Lieutenant?"

"It's Mrs. Jones's BMW, Mr. Owens."

"What!?"

He found more photographs.

"And here are more photos of your very recognizable Plymouth Fury and her little, white, equally recognizable BMW together at your various tournaments," he said, handing over the additional photographs.

"What?!" I repeated, taking them, handing the others to Buonorotti.

"This file and these photographs are the record Mr. Jones kept of what he seems to believe was an affair you were having with Mrs. Jones. He also has a record of dates and encounters. He even apparently recorded," and here he looked especially carefully at both Buonorotti and me. "Some of your assignations. He figured out how to turn on the mic on his wife's phone. As well as her GPS."

"What?!"

"Yep," Lunt exhaled.

"I mean, what … does 'assignations' mean?"

"An assignation is a get-together, so to speak, during an illicit affair."

"So, like, sex?"

"That's right."

"Assignations, Buonorotti."

"I did not know the word myself, Oose."

"Don't feel bad, Buonorotti. You're not a native speaker."

Lunt's eyes went back and forth between us. Then he wiggled a bit in his chair and took out a small SD card.

"This camera card has recordings Mr. Jones made. He claims in his notes that the recording includes his wife's voice. She says 'Oh, Oose!' on multiple occasions and in a somewhat, how does one express it, overwrought manner."

"What?!"

"It goes on for an hour."

"An hour?"

I turned to Buonorotti, who gave me a complimentary nod.

"It's an altogether quite compelling case for a divorce," Lunt said. "His attorney told us that they'd been working on it for months, though he hadn't seen the file himself. We found it in Mr. Jones's car. His notes also indicate that Mrs. Jones in fact ran back to him. From you."

"From me back to him?"

"The notes seem to indicate she eventually realized how much she loved Bowdoin. That is, Mr. Jones. Maybe she got tired or even," Lunt again added some looks. "Frightened of you."

"What?"

"These notes say you got jealous and angry about losing her."

"There's a lot of information in those notes!"

"So," Lunt said. "You're saying that none of this is true?"

"None of it!" I said. "Not a word! Is there even a picture of me with either of them in there?"

"There's this one, yes," Lunt said, handing over a picture of me. "You seem to be smiling, kissing, and you have your hand on her chest."

"What?" I looked at it. "Wait! That was taken yesterday!"

"Oh, yeah?" Lunt said, reclaiming the picture and returning it to the file.

"They're clearly setting me up!"

"Right," Lunt said.

"And I certainly didn't commit any assignations!"

"I see."

"I think I'd remember assigning a woman like that!"

Lunt nodded, pushing himself up on one haunch to draw out a big iPhone.

"If you would, Mr. Owens," Lunt said. "Explain this."

He turned his phone to share a video of me and Bowdoin Jones fighting on the pier.

"She drove me down there to surveil her cheating husband, like I said! She hired me last night! That's as long as I've known her! She hired me, drove me down there, told me to watch his boat, then her husband jumped out of the bushes and attacked me!"

"What were you arguing about?"

"I wasn't arguing!" I said. "He was! Jones! It was completely bizarre! He jumped me, started grabbing me, then hopped in a little dingy and raced out to the boat. Can't you see this is a set up?!"

"A set up ..."

"Look, Lunt," I said. "I don't want to do your job for you, but who took that video? It's jumping all around. Clearly it's not some surveillance system."

"Perhaps," Lunt said, giving a gopher-ish sniff.

"Are you accusing me of murder?"

"No," he said. "It's a missing persons case at this point."

"Because you don't have a body?"

"Not yet," he said, ominously, then scribbled something in his notebook.

Watching him scribble, my investigative instincts started getting antsy. This happens. Friends, family, various institutions and notable experts have long agreed on my low mental acuity, yet in this PI line of work, I have occasional, penetrating insights. Regretfully, they tend to override my other circuits and shoot directly out of my mouth.

"There must have been other boats damaged," I heard myself half-ask, half-state.

Lunt came back up from his notebook.

"That's right," he said. "Two other boats were destroyed."

"Destroyed?"

"Flaming material cast into the air by the explosion landed in the sails of the other boats. Being made of wood, the hulls caught fire. The fires descended to the engine rooms and blew up the gas tanks."

"What were boats' names?"

"The Big Short was one, a 40-foot friendship sloop. The other was Tranche du Paradis. A Hylas H46."

"Was anyone on the Big Short or the Tranche do whatchamacallit?"

"No."

"But of course you're sure that Bowdoin Jones was on The Flustered Lush."

"You just said yourself that you saw him motoring out to it," Lunt parried.

"Yes," I said. Dang it!

"Okay," Lunt said. He wrote something else in his notebook.

"This is a massive set-up, Lunt!"

"Well, we'll find out. Play the rest of your tournament, Mr. Owens," Lunt said, adding a twitch of smile. "It'll keep you around. I'm sure we'll be in touch before it's over."

He nodded at me, then Buonorotti, and exited stage left.

I smiled with irrepressible cheer. Buonorotti watched me from a chair in the corner.

"He'll make this interesting," I said, once Lunt was well on his way. "And fun. Pudgy, angry, hairy little guy like that!"

"The police have a powerful case against you, Oose."

"Yes!" I said, clapping my hands together and rubbing them vigorously. I may have even bobbed my eyebrows. "Did you pick up on that crock about the other boats? That pause he did, then the eye twitch?"

"No," Buonorotti answered, curious.

"You didn't? He did it twice."

"Two twitches?"

"Two twitches, Buonorotti. In Salem in 1640, two twitches were enough to send you right to the stake!"

"There is much to think carefully about. What is the meaning of the multiple boats?"

"I don't know! It means something, but I don't want to think about it. In fact, let's not think about anything at all. You see how I started thinking, and BAM I came up with that multiple-boats thing? And the presence of another person taking that video?"

"Keen insights, Oose."

"Thanks! So! I take you home. We both nap, shower, primp, preen and then I'll give you a lift back here to the Players' Dinner. Jacket required, Buonorotti! And rule number one: No thinking!"

Soon, we were side by side again in the glorious Plymouth Fury, rolling through the dappled evening sunlight and coastline.

I was similarly radiant and struggling not to laugh. Or sing another song. After a while, however, I couldn't help but register Buonorotti's silence.

"What's up?" I said loudly, since we were driving alfresco. "Are you thinking, Buonorotti? Because we agreed explicitly not to think."

"Well," he said, lifting a hand. "I will admit, it's difficult not to consider that you are a suspect in a murder investigation, Oose. At the very least, it should affect your game."

"It should, shouldn't it!" I giggled. "Yeah, but instead I'm gonna play out of my mind!"

"And the police ... well, I don't know how it is in this country, but sometimes in Italy they are quite happy to put anyone in jail, just to say they solved the crime."

"Same thing here, Buonorotti! With the added complication of Lunt being up to something. Of course, I refuse to think about what that something might be."

"But what if he puts you in jail, Oose," he said. "I have been in jails. They are no place for straight men who wear pink pants."

"I don't doubt it. But again, Buonorotti, you're thinking."

"Ah, yes. Forgive me."

"When the time comes, right around Sunday, we'll figure all that out," I said with a dismissive wave. "People who do this sort of thing, set up guys like me to take a fall? They're dumb! They're desperate! Add to that the heightened emotion and stress of a nutty crime like this, and it gets even easier for us to figure out what happened."

"Why is that, Oose?"

"Because there's a million mistakes they can make," I continued. "That they've probably already made. And clearly it's a set up. They'd clearly heard I was in this PI racket and thought it made me especially vulnerable."

"That suggests they gave the matter a considerable amount of thought, Oose."

"And they don't even have a body! Take some solace in that, Buonorotti," I added, concluding the discussion.

Dinner was a predictable country club affair. A beef option, a chicken option, a big lump of starch and an overdone, though colorful, selection of vegetables. A bite or two, then onto the booze. The basic idea and intent, I'm sure.

After that, we milled about the bar with the other golf types. I confess I was beaming, and all too happy to share stories and allow myself to be over-served. At one point, however, when there was a pause in the action, Buonorotti leaned into me.

"Oose," he began. "I really do think you should do some kind of PI investigating."

"Blahh ..." I countered.

"It's never good to be the primary suspect in something, Oose," he observed. "I have been a primary suspect in many things."

Something about the term "primary suspect," I will admit, did strike me as ominous.

"What do you propose I do?"

"Well," he said, after a moment's consideration and substantial frowning. "You seemed to think it was unusual for two other boats to explode."

"Yes?"

"Maybe you ask the bartender, 'Bartender, do you know who owns these other exploded boats?'"

"That *is* a good idea, Buonorotti."

"Thank you, Oose."

"You sure you weren't some kind of PI at some point?"

"No. I was a priest. And a boxer. A legionnaire. Never a, as you say, PI."

"Hmm," I said. "Well. It's a good idea nonetheless!"

I happened to be leaning on the bar at the time, so it was the work of an instant to pivot on my elbow and look for the bartender. A stroke of luck put him right in front of me. There were perhaps ten inches between our foreheads.

"Excuse me," I began, twirling a drink. "I'll have another one of these. And also, you wouldn't by any chance know the names of the guys — or gals — whose boats blew up this morning?"

"Sure," he answered, working the cola gun. "One of them's right over there. Burt Madden."

He threw his head to his left, which didn't help me too much.

"Which one is Madden?"

"The one who can't stop laughing."

And there he was. With one hand, he was clutching some fat guy's shoulder. With another he was swinging his own drink around. He was in fact laughing. So much so, I could count all his teeth.

"He seems happy."

"Wouldn't you be?" the bartender asked, gathering up the drinks.

"But his boat blew up."

"Exactly. Half the people here dream of the day that their boats blow up."

"Really?"

He could see I didn't quite get it.

"Boats are like black holes for your money," he said. "They just suck it all in. Look at the guys around him. Look at all that envy and resentment. They think Burt won the lottery. Sure, they pretend like it doesn't matter to them, but it does."

Sure enough, a quick study of the surrounding faces revealed significant degrees of envy and resentment. These feelings only diminished slightly when Madden let out a cackle so energetic it turned him red as turnip and he seemed briefly on the verge of a heart attack.

"If you have something to hide, Buonorotti, like knowledge beforehand that someone intends to blow up your boat, would you behave like this guy?"

"I do not think so, Oose."

"Me neither. So, Burt Madden here probably had no idea this was going to happen."

"So it would seem."

I slapped the bar.

"Dang it, we're thinking, Buonorotti!"

"I'm sorry, Oose."

I tried to refocus.

"Alright, we gotta shake this off. I'm gonna have another drink, then let's review today's round. Did you have any thoughts on how I played today?"

This was a mistake on my part, as Buonorotti had considerable thoughts on how I played today, many of which had almost nothing to do with the game of golf, at least in my analysis. It should be remembered that we barely knew one another at this point. Further, Buonorotti had yet to completely unburden himself of his Demon Goddess of Golf philosophical system.

"Oose, Golf is like a beautiful woman," he said at one point, laying the groundwork. "To win, you must woo her with your game. With the allure of your game. As such, you cannot say these things like … ah … 'We are all going down …'"

He searched for the rest of the phrase.

"'*We* all going down …'" I corrected him.

"'We all going down … to the Stinkytown,' which I believe you said on the 15th hole."

"'*We* all goin' down to *Stankytown*' is the actual phrase, Buonorotti."

"And what," he said, squinting. "What is in Stinkytown."

"It's an expression is what it is."

"And what does it express?"

"It doesn't express anything!"

"Oh. But Oose an expression should …"

"It expresses that I just smoked some wild-ass shot!"

"I see."

"And it's so hot it stinks!"

"It heated up to a degree that it is stinky."

"Precisely!"

"I am no scientist, Oose, but …"

"… but that's how hot a shot it was, Buonorotti, and it's making everyone stink it's so hot. We stunk. Both of us. We stunk good because that shot was so hot!"

"Now, Oose, in what world would you ever say such a thing to a beautiful woman? And I shouldn't have to add that these are the things I asked you specifically not to say. That was our agreement."

He made further observations, and it was only by the sheer force of luck that I escaped. A number of young women had appeared and seemed to lock onto Buonorotti, popping up among the crowd and staring at him like the Children of the Corn. When I indicated such to him, he quickly replaced his sunglasses — this seemed to be the only way he could smother his smoldering sexual appeal. In this instance, he was too late, and he felt the need to move briskly for the men's room. The young women followed, accelerating on converging trajectories, and actually colliding with one another at the men's room door.

I took the opportunity to huddle up with some of the other golf jocks. As is usually the case, several pace-setters were ushering the rest through a few rounds of hilarious stories. There were spit-takes, imitation swings, indexing of hot chicks in the gallery, trays of drinks coming and going and pretty soon it was practically midnight.

I don't recall exactly what brought me out onto the balcony or why it was so completely empty when I got there. Perhaps I was merely taking a break. It was a wondrous summer night. The stars were like a fine dust in the black sky. The golf course below seemed like my own private kingdom.

I savored the moment, reflecting on my mad, little life. My empty list of accomplishments, my empty bank account. My ex-wives. My iron play. Ah, what a world, I recall thinking. Such beauty. Such mystery. A surprise around every corner.

Ironically, just such a surprise presented itself to me, and at that very moment. And as far as surprises go, it was substantial, being both auditory and tactile, if that's the right word. Multi-dimensional is probably the term I want here. My point is that I both heard something ("Hi, Oozy, baby …") and felt something (a set of ice cold fingers traveling around my waist from behind and diving toward the particulars).

"Jiminy H. Christmas!" I announced, spinning, hopping, retucking my clothes and transitioning from a mood of mellow philosophy to that of a jackrabbit on cocaine.

"Hi," Jiggly Jones said. "It's just me … the bereaved!"

She said it with a light, devilish laugh, a laugh that was somehow infuriating, outrageous and terribly sexy all at once.

"Jiggly!?! What are you doing here?"

"You're cute, Oozy, honey," she said, trying to help me with my shirt. "In a colorful, goofy, loud, little way."

"STOP IT!"

I managed to disentangle myself and push her back. She seemed to welcome the break and set a hand on her hip. Her perfect hip, I should add, bound tightly by her tiny, perfect skirt. With her other hand, she held up a glass of champagne. She'd placed herself in a circle of moonlight that seemed somehow unnatural. Otherworldly. Like it followed her everywhere!

"I wanted to let you know, Oozy," she said, lifting her champagne flute. "That you have absolutely nothing to worry about. It's all a sham! Bowdoin's fine. We faked his death!"

"You did."

"We had to. Just like we had to set you up."

"Had to?"

"Had to! And believe me, we promise we'll make it up to you. See, Bowdoin made a tiny mistake with the fund he was managing. Everybody freaked out. They're all like *Where's my money! I'm wiped out! I lost everything!* But actually, it happens all the time. And they're all loaded anyway. And his college roommate made a tiny mistake with his fund and had to fake his death, too. But it's all okay now! In fact, he's better than okay. He's managing an even bigger fund today! And some of the people got most of their money back!"

"But you're sure Bowdoin's alive and didn't go up in the explosion?"

She paused to consider me. Then she clicked her tongue and slowly shook her head.

"You're really worried about Bowdoin, aren't you?"

"Not really!"

She'd closed, setting her fingers on my arm.

"Cute and compassionate," she whispered. "Bowdoin's fine, Ooze."

She kept looking at me, into one eye, then another. Desperate to focus elsewhere, I locked in on her outfit, as little of it as there was.

"You know you may want to wear something different," I heard myself say.

"Don't you like what I'm wearing?" she asked, sparkling her eyes.

"Oh, I do. I do. Just, probably, as a thought, you should maybe wear less clingy, shimmery, slinky stuff."

"Oh," she said, then pouted, as if I'd hurt her feelings.

I quickly added, "I mean, you are in mourning, your husband's supposed to be dead, but you seem to not even be wearing any ..."

My mouth seized up. What was I saying!?

"Any what?"

"..."

"Underwear?"

"No!"

"No, Oozy?"

"No! NO. No, no, no. SOCKS!"

"Is that what you're asking, Oozy? Am I wearing underwear?"

"Noooo. I meant socks!"

"I am not wearing socks."

"Good!"

"Or underwear."

"OK!" I managed, then changed subjects. "Where is Bowdoin now?!"

"I don't know, actually," she said, a squall of frustration passing in her eyes. "We had a rendezvous point ..."

"And he didn't show up?"

"That's right. That's actually why I've got the sexy outfit on. He's crazy jealous, so when I tramp around a bit, he usually shows up quick. And madder than a hornet!"

"But you're sure he's alive?"

"Sure, I'm sure! It would take more than a boat explosion to kill Bowdoin Jones."

"Actually, there were three boat explosions," I said.

"What?"

"Or rather, three boats were totaled as part of the explosion on the Flustered Lush."

"What?!"

"Yeah, three boats were destroyed, including the Flustered Lush."

"Three boats," she said to herself, then again to me. "Three boats?"

"Three boats," I confirmed.

"That son of a ...," she said, heating up like a teapot. "I'll bet he's up to something!"

"Like what?"

"He absolutely is! That fat, crafty, gambling dingleberry!"

"You're talking about your husband?"

"Always trying to make money with some crazy new angle!"

"He's got another angle? On top of faking his own death?"

"He's probably going to collect insurance money on those boats! Or at least a commission!"

"How?"

"And if he thinks he can cut me out, he's got another thing coming!"

She downed the rest of her champagne, turned and smashed her glass against the wall.

"Bankers!" she cried.

And with that, she was gone.

CHAPTER FOUR — FRIDAY

I remained stunned and inert for perhaps five minutes. Only when a pair of young lovers appeared on the porch and began to canoodle did I recover. Pushing my way back inside, a lively fan base welcomed me, and soon I was again surrounded by back-slappers and drink-buyers. It wasn't long before I was back on track, telling hilarious stories, describing key course management decisions and tracing brilliant shots with my hands, very much like a fighter pilot recounting aerial combat. Jiggly Jones and my significant legal jeopardy temporarily receded into the background.

With a professional's regard for the challenges of the next day, I left early, retrieving Buonorotti and returning us to our respective hotels. En route, I recounted to him my encounter with Jiggly Jones, and his grim reception of the details was hard to interpret. At first, I thought I had alarmed him to the degree that he was speechless. But that seemed hard to imagine. This, of course, was still the very earliest days of our relationship. It would be much later that I'd realize his silence was an indication of his monomania: he was thinking exclusively about the round tomorrow. There are times when he descends into a kind of alternate reality.

"She's sassy and crazy and rich and criminal and gorgeous and psychotic, all with this kind of Barbara Eden vibe," I said. "Did you ever encounter a woman like that, Buonorotti? I mean, in your adventures as an underwear model?"

"I think tomorrow will be less humid," he replied. "The ball will carry perhaps five or even six percent further."

"Did you even get 'I Dream of Genie' in Italy?"

"You'll want Pro V-1s with the additional dimples. For control. The Pro-V1xs have an inadequate number of dimples."

"Inadequate dimples?"

"I think our balls may have too many dimples, Oose."

"How do you even know how many dimples our balls have, Buonorotti?"

"I know these things."

The funny thing is, he was looking right at me, and responding as if he thought his replies made perfect sense. Of course, I was driving too fast to permit much if any conversation. He to his hotel, me to mine, and thus the first day of the tournament ended.

We arrived early the next tournament morning (Friday), and I parked in my preferred corner. The first thing we noticed were the ranks of supercars — McLarens, Lamborghinis, Ferraris, Vipers. It was nothing new to me, sad to say, but it did surprise Buonorotti.

"Where did all these fancy cars come from, Oose?"

"Tour guys, Buonorotti," I said. "They know I'm on a roll and want in on the action."

"Gambling?"

"Gambling."

"How did they get these cars here, Oose?"

"Flew 'em in," I answered. "On those planes the Army uses to transport tanks."

"I see."

"In the end, golf is about gambling, Buonorotti," I explained. "And the top Tour guys gamble like anybody else. In fact, they want to be as renown and dangerous gambling as they are playing. Some merely because they like it. Some, because they don't want to look weak. Others, because they're addicts. A select few because it's yet another way to lord their talent over others."

"That is very interesting, Oose, and entirely surprising to me, I should emphasize. And these Tour guys know about you?"

"They know all about me, Buonorotti," I said. "The last time I lit it up like this, I broke two course records in a row, shooting a consecutive 58 and 59. The whole tour is handicapped, even at this level, and my win blew out the odds. Only one person bet on me that tournament. The biggest gambler of them all. Codename: California King. Sometimes Chief Pale Head. Or Mel Fincklestein. His real name, of course, is Wink Paddington."

Buonorotti grabbed my clubs from the back seat and hoisted them on his shoulder.

"Are you saying Wink Paddington is here, Oose?"

I looked over the cars, then out to sea.

"He is here, Buonorotti," I said. "I can sense his presence. There is a disturbance in the Force."

"It is your PI instinct, Oose."

"Yeah, well, it is like the Force at times, Buonorotti."

I marched up the small hill, through a gazebo-type thing and then to an outdoor buffet for the tournament breakfast. We ran the gauntlet of other players. The Tour guys dotted the crowd like little galaxies, radiating glory and orbited by their handlers, women and the other fawning semi-pros. They all, however, turned to watch me enter.

I tipped a cap to a few I knew for one reason or another. Somehow, I felt up-to-my-eyeballs in confidence.

"Oy! Owens! OY!" we heard behind us, loud and nasally. That was followed by, "What, What, What!"

I turned to find fish-faced Cocky Brill bouncing on his heels.

"Cocky," I said.

His eyes lit up.

"U.S.," he said, then looked both ways. Like a rat with a dirty joke. "California King is here."

"Is that right," I said, giving Buonorotti a look.

"It is."

"How'd he find out?"

"I told him!"

I snorted my response.

Cocky's gaze left me and moved to Buonorotti.

"Now," Cocky said, as his eyes went wider and fishier. "Just the man I wanted to see. What's your name then, mate?"

"My name?"

"Right, you bloody name, innit, what?"

"My name is Giancarlo Scillaci Buonorotti."

"Washyer real name, en?"

"That is my real name."

"No, mate. It ain't," Cocky sniffed, thought and arrived at his conclusion. "I know you."

"I don't think so," Buonorotti said.

"I *know* you," Cocky said, then leaned in. "From *somewhere*."

"Again, I do not think so."

"I think I do. I think I'm gonna make some inquiries. With the right people. In the right channoos. Oy! Look over there, Ey!"

His fishy eyes swung off Buonorotti's shoulder. He pointed. We turned to look.

"What?" I said, looking out the window.

"Oh," Cocky said. "I thought I saw a bald eagle, mate. My mistake!"

Now we swung back to him. He was smiling. He was also holding his phone in Buonorotti's face.

"Say cheese!"

"Formaggio?"

Cocky took his picture.

"Yeah, mate! You fell right into my trap, innit? I'm gonna send this picture to this guy I know who knows things about things, mate! What? Right!"

Before we could respond, Cocky took off, bolting through the door and bounding over shrubs like a gazelle.

"Who do you think he thinks you are?"

"I do not know, Oose."

"Maybe Cocky has the hunk-of-the-month calendar, too," I mused.

I breezed through the front side with a whimsical four under. On Nine, a sharp dogleg left, I sent a towering three iron over the trees, then bent it, catching the fairway downgrade for an extra fifty yards of roll. 280 yards total for an easy seven iron in, which I spun back and left within a foot of the hole. With a seven iron. Downhill. I smile even as I write these words. And thank God Buonorotti was there, because my original read on the green made him stare at me for perhaps five seconds. On a foot-long putt!

Ten is a dogleg right, but doesn't turn until 200 yards out. I took out Screaming Eagle, spoke to her a bit, and we agreed that she would stay low and straight until about 20 yards shy of the trees, at which point she would start an easy fade. And so she did, like a guided freaking golf missile.

I took a birdie on 10, another on 11, another on 12.

And then we arrived at 13, where Buonorotti and I had our first in a series of Difficult Exchanges.

We'd arrived at the tee box, and I inspected the sun dazzled fairway with my steely glare. 13 descends at a steep grade, then doglegs left. For a player at the height of his powers, it's irresistible to go high, over the trees, and even draw it a bit, all of which I'd done both Wednesday and Thursday. On Wednesday, I'd dropped my tee shot 20 feet from the green.

So, it was with firm confidence that I called over my shoulder.

"A four iron, please."

"NNNNNHHhhhhhnnnnnnnnno," I heard.

"What?" I said, turning.

"Not the four, Oose. There is too much humidity today. It would be difficult to carry the trees."

"Too much humidity?"

"I think straight out, with a low flight. Perhaps your six, with something taken off of it."

"I'm gonna hit the four," I said, wide-eyed, a bit scandalized.

"No, you are not."

"Who are you, my mother?!"

"Remember our arrangement. You will do everything I say."

"You weren't serious!"

"I was very much the serious person."

"Why?"

"Do you want the golf answer or the spiritual answer?"

"The golf, NO, the spiritual answer!"

"The goddess of golf is daring you to hit the four. She may even let you succeed with such a shot."

"So what's the freaking problem!?"

"But she is setting you up, my friend. Like a cruel, but beautiful woman might set up a homely little friend, purely for her own amusement."

"And I'm the friend?"

"That was purely an illustration. Here is another illustration that may help you: consider … a crazy ex-wife, yes?"

"Alright?"

"A crazy ex-wife who invites you over for some happy reason," he said and looked over his lenses. "The age old happy reason."

"Uh-huh?"

"But you know, deep down," he said. "There are no such happy reasons."

"Hmm ..."

"Don't you?"

"Ehnn ..."

"You do know that, Oose."

"The goddess of golf is a crazy ex-wife ..." I said, speculatively.

"You are beginning to understand, I think."

He took out the six. He handed it to me.

"We will quiet your game, Oose. The goddess of golf will forget all about us, and then we will win."

"Right ..." I said, taking the six.

"Straight out, please, Oose."

I hit it straight out. I took a par on 13.

I bristled through 14 and 15. The exchanges between myself and Buonorotti remained as frosty as a frozen banana. Still, I took his direction, and my play stayed on target, if maddeningly pedestrian. It was only the sight of squad cars at the clubhouse that resurrected my spirits.

"The cops are back!"

"That's very good news, Oose."

My eyes darted about in thought.

"Something's happened!" I realized.

"You should keep your focus on the golfing, Oose. A drive here, with a hint of a fade, I should think."

"I can't help it sometimes. My mind starts racing ahead. It's these razor sharp PI instincts! If I figure out how to get myself out of this mess, I'm screwed!"

"That is not good," Buonorotti said. "For your golfing."

"Quick! Tell me a story, Buonorotti!"

"A story about what, Oose?"

"I don't know. You're the underwear model!"

"That," he said, with his brief frown. "As you know, it is not something I prefer to talk about ..."

"... yeah, well, stuff that in the turkey hole! I'm taking orders here like an organ grinder's monkey," I said, and I'm afraid I added a bit of an illustrative dance. "The least you could do is humor me a bit with a story!"

He swung his jaw around in consideration, then said, eventually:

"I did live briefly with an Aragonese Countess in a castle in the Pyrenees."

"That is exactly the kind of story I was looking for, Buonorotti!"

"I have a scar across my back from the Count of Zaragustia."

"And that's related to the Countess story?"

"He was her husband."

"Excellent. What kind of scar?"

"A saber scar."

"Uh-huh. Do it. Tell the story!"

He removed his glasses and looked off into the distance. His hair lifted in the wind.

"The real story, Oose," he said. "Was the Countess."

"What about the Countess? Was she smoking hot?"

"She was beautiful."

"Give me a description. Beautiful doesn't cut it. This golf course is beautiful. A woman is …"

"A woman is … another matter. You are right, Oose," he said, and I could see him thinking. "I hope it doesn't sound boastful, but I have been among the most beautiful women in the world. As a fashion model."

"As a European fashion model, there were a lot of hot female European fashion models around, you're saying."

"Just so."

"Wow!" I said, trying to lean into it a bit, even as I saw a couple cops fiddling around in the distance.

"Nevertheless, this woman, the Countess, was the most beautiful woman I have ever seen. The eyes of a wild Moor. Skin a shade of the Andalusian desert."

"Curvy?"

"Yes, but artfully so."

"Leggy?"

"Quite long legs. Those of a huntress."

"Yikes!"

"She grew up a peasant near Granada. By the time she was fifteen, she was famous throughout the valley for her astonishing beauty. So much so that she would disguise herself when she visited the village, so she wouldn't drive the local men mad. Soon not even that would work, and she was forced to travel only at night."

"Wow!"

"One such night, returning home from her prayers at the Catedral, her father told her an incredible story: she wasn't their child at all — she was in actuality a princess hidden and raised as their own to protect her from a vicious, generation's old vendetta. He said that her hand in marriage had been promised to the head of another aristocratic family, the Count of Zaragustia, upon the death of her real parents. Her real mother had died long ago. Her real father, a baron, had been struck down in a duel that very day, a victim of that age-old vendetta. The Count of Zaragustia would come to claim her in the morning."

"Wow! Did she believe she was a princess?"

"She believed her father sold her to this Count."

"Excellent. Keep going!"

"She was at that time in love with a boy from her village. She thought her father had sold her to the Count to keep her from this boy."

"And to make money, right?"

"It is so," Buonorotti said. "The next morning, the Count arrived. The princess tried to resist, but the Count would not be refused. Five hundred miles they traveled, from Granada to the Aragonese high country, but at every turn, the Count looked back."

"Lost?"

"He feared this peasant boy who loved the princess. The Count had seen him as they left their village. There was something in the boy's eyes he didn't like. A seven iron here, Oose."

"Seven? I was going to go low with a six."

"No, we must quiet your game."

"I could stick it … well, whatever! Fine. Gimme the seven."

I took my swing. It was flawless. The ball tumbled to the center of the green.

"So this Count whisks her away to this castle?" I said, handing back the seven.

"He does, but at every turn, he sees this boy. And so the Count starts doubling back. Changing carriages. Horses. Cars. Trains, all to elude this young man. Finally, when he sees the boy no more, the Count takes her to his castle. A castle of seven towers, high in the Pyrenees."

"Good luck busting into that joint, handsome peasant boy!"

"Indeed, Oose, indeed. The Count arranged a secret ceremony."

"Smart."

"But the princess refused her vows. The Count made the priest record the marriage anyway. That night, the princess became his Countess."

"Wow! Where do you come in, Buonorotti?"

"I was her gigolo."

It should be noted that this was the first time Buonorotti revealed this side of his career to me.

"Her what now?"

"Her gigolo, Oose. A kind of hired lover."

"I know what a gigolo is. I just wasn't sure I heard you properly. You were a gigolo, you're saying?"

"You understand me perfectly."

"A *gigolo*."

"Exactly, Oose."

"I see," I said, then said it one more time, still a bit stunned. "You were a gigolo, you're saying."

"Precisely, Oose. Every night, beneath the starry Spanish heavens, we would make love in each of the seven towers."

"In every tower?"

"Is true."

"Seven towers?"

"The Seven Towered Castle of the Count of Zaragustia, yes."

"Wow," I gulped.

"It was a question of duty."

"As a gigolo?"

"Indeed. When the Count hired me ..."

"He hired you?"

"Yes. He was away quite often," he said. "He had a significant interest in shipping. The Count stayed in Dakar much of the year. He also hoped perhaps that I would make her forget about the peasant boy."

"I'll bet! Seven times a night!"

"Putt it here, please, Oose."

"Oh, right!" I drained it. "Keep going!"

"One evening, in the aftermath of our passionate embrace, she told me she loved me," Buonorotti said. He paused here before resuming. "No one had ever said these words to me before. I realized I loved her as well. For one wonderful summer, we lived as lovers would. In a castle. In the Pyrenees. In our towers."

"So what happened? How the hell did you get the scar?"

"Our love became a scandal known throughout the valley. It was impossible to keep from the Count, even on the other side of the world."

"The internet?"

"I would not doubt that the internet played some role."

"Or texting!"

"Yes," he said. "Enraged to learn that we were in love, the Count came home. One night, amidst torrential rain, heat, and a terrifying electrical storm, he burst into our room as we made love."

"No!"

"I never saw him. I heard only thunder. I saw only lightning. I heard my adored Countess scream and took it for a cry of passion. That's when I felt the saber carve through the sinews of my back."

"Ouch!"

"Traveling like a serpent through my skin, from my left shoulder to my right hip. I fell over in pain to find the Count over me, his eyes pushing out his skull, the saber high and gleaming in the moonlight. I was defenseless. I, a legionnaire … a gap wedge here, Oose."

"Huh?"

"A gap wedge. A full swing."

"Sure," I said and dropped it on the green. "Well? What happened?"

"There was another deafening sound. The Count's chest burst open. A bloom of bloody tissue. He'd been shot."

"The peasant boy!"

"The same. The Count had evaded the peasant boy for years, but after he'd secured us in the Castle of the Seven Towers, the Count resumed his normal life … and the peasant boy resumed following him. Still, the Count had always been careful to take evasive measures when he traveled home. This time, enraged by the love between the Countess and me, he came directly back. The boy, her true love, followed. My Countess had used me. She created the charade of our love to outrage the Count, inspire the rumor mongers of the village and lead the boy right to her. Their love was so great that it eclipsed that between the Countess and me. If you can say that she and I were ever in love at all."

"Why didn't the peasant boy kill you, too?"

"She wouldn't let him. They took me to a hospital and disappeared forever."

"Did you get any money?"

"She tried to give me money, but I wouldn't take it. It was beneath my dignity."

"Your dignity as a gigolo?"

"And my true, undying love for the Countess."

"Wow!"

"Here is your read, Oose."

"What's that now? Oh."

I putted in. The crowd roared. A crowd I hadn't even noticed, including the cops and, in the center of them all, Lieutenant Lunt. Buonorotti plucked my ball out of the 18th hole.

"That was an eagle, Oose."

"Was it?"

"A very quiet eagle. For a very quiet 59," he said, taking the putter and cleaning it up. "We will only play better tomorrow."

Lunt started waddling our way.

I refocused on Buonorotti.

"Show me the scar," I said to Buonorotti, feeling a twitch of a smile on my lips.

"I will do so later, Oose," he said.

"You do have a scar, don't you, Buonorotti?"

"Of course."

"Of course," I said and pivoted. "Lieutenant Lunt, what a nice surprise!"

"Good afternoon," Lunt said. "We just dragged a dead body out of the ocean. You're both under arrest for the murder of Bowdoin Jones."

"You just dragged this guy out of the water, Lunt?!" I guffawed, as Buonorotti and I were frog-marched to our jail cell. "And you're already convinced it's Bowdoin Jones and that he was murdered? By me?!"

"We have your assault of Mr. Jones two nights ago."

I guffawed again.

"We also have Mr. Jones's file on you," Lunt added. "As well as all that video."

"How'd you even know it was him? Bowdoin Jones was probably a big hunk of wet charcoal!"

"He was, mostly," Lunt said. "With the exception of his right arm, which had a tattoo."

"Of what?"

"An anchor."

"An anchor tattoo? On a banker, Lunt?"

"That's right. We know he had one. His wife said so."

"Where'd you find him?"

"Newcomb's Head."

"Where's that?"

"Just above Newcomb's Neck."

Lunt's mustache gave the briefest twitch of satisfaction.

"Good one, chief," the deputy said.

"What is this? The Gong Show? Has our bail been set?"

"Fifty grand a piece."

"And you realize, of course, that I'll be out of here in less than an hour, tops? With all the money riding on me right now?"

"All the more reason to have a seat and relax, Owens," Lunt said. "I think we're done with the knowledge exchange."

The deputy slid home the bars. Lunt started down the hall.

"What about my phone call, Lunt!?"

"Here's a phone, Owens," the deputy said, producing one out of nowhere. "One call."

I noticed his name tag.

"You're a Lunt, too?"

He didn't answer, but wagged a finger at the phone. I studied him more closely.

"Didn't I see you at the Sennetts Harbor Club last night?"

"I work nights there. Make your call."

"Right," I said, giving Deputy Lunt a final once-over, then cradling the handset on my shoulder. "One call for Buonorotti, too."

"There is no one I could call, Oose."

"Jeez, Buonorotti," I said, giving both him and the deputy a look. "Are you trying to depress everybody?"

With my one phone call, I left a message for my golf bookie friend, Bill Parker. He didn't pick up so I left a message. One rarely likes to leave a message with one's only call from jail, but under the circumstances, knowing I was the focal point of millions of dollars of gambling action, I was without worry. A guy like Bill, with his fat rolodex of world class douchebags, would take care of everything.

And that was that. The deputy took the phone and disappeared. Buonorotti and I occupied benches opposite one another. The cool tang of sea air drifted in from the window above us, giving our incarceration some modest dignity.

"Fifty grand," I smirked. "We'll be out of here in an hour. Maybe less."

"I do not doubt it, Oose."

I took the opportunity to study Buonorotti. Most men, upon landing in a jail cell, freak out. Buonorotti seemed entirely at ease, passing through his variety of philosophical, European expressions. For a while he squinted at the window. For another few minutes, he seemed spacey, lips parted, but somehow still deeply thoughtful — a distracted genius. Then he moved on to something wide-eyed and crazy, then to a kind of secret amusement.

"You've been in a jail before, haven't you, Buonorotti?"

"Yes."

"Tell me about it."

"I was on Devil's Island."

"Right, right. What for?"

"I killed a man in Marseilles," Buonorotti sighed. "I told him not to try to kill me, but he did try and I killed him. I wish it were a better story, Oose."

"That reminds me. Show me the saber scar, if you would."

I half-expected some outlandish excuse. Instead, Buonorotti simply turned and pulled up the back of his shirt. A long, diagonal ridge of puffy tissue snaked from his shoulder to his waist. He pulled the shirt back down and faced me.

"The brand of gigolo," he said.

"I'm almost buying it," I said.

"It is also, if you'll allow me, the scar where the Princess opened me up," he said. "To break my heart."

"Women," I said. "Speaking of which, do you actually believe all this Demon Goddess of Golf razz-mattazz?"

"I believe in little else, Oose."

"Huh," I said.

A dozen, deafening clicks and clanks filled the room. The jail door opened.

"There we are," I said, standing.

The deputy entered.

"Owens? Buonorotti?" he said. "You're free to go."

The deputy ushered us to the front. We were handed our various things.

"Who sprung us?" I asked the deputy. "Just for the record?"

He didn't answer. Instead he sorta nodded toward the front. I didn't get it at first, then I noticed the other deputy, who seemed frozen in a kind of sci-fi shock, his fingers hovering over his keyboard. I followed his line of sight into the lobby. A young woman fiddled carelessly with brochures mounted on a wall. She wore a glittery kerchief around her head, huge sunglasses, and a short raincoat. Or should I say, a short, see-through raincoat, allowing one to see through to — there's really no other word for it — a bra. The raincoat itself, meanwhile, ended right around her waist, revealing the briefest pair of shorts, if they could be so defined, and million dollar legs. One was left with the impression that she'd tried to disguise herself, then decided to reverse course about half way.

"Jiggly?" I said, approaching. "Did you bail us out?"

"I did, Oozy, honey!" she said, then closed, grabbed my rump and kissed me. "I didn't want you not to have the opportunity to finish such a great round of golf!"

"Thanks," I managed. "Wait! Where'd you get the money? I thought you were more or less broke?"

"I talked to some boat owners."

"And they just gave you fifty grand?"

"Men are always giving me money."

"Really?"

"Yeah!"

Buonorotti joined us. I felt my rump spring free.

"Who's your friend?" Jiggly asked, with an added, but slight note of sudden huskiness.

"My name is Giancarlo Scillaci Buonorotti. I am Mr. Owens's caddy," he said, taking her hand.

"Giancarlo …" she answered.

"It is a great pleasure to meet a truly lovely woman."

"Oooh," she purred.

"He was an underwear model," I felt it necessary to add.

"So was I!"

"In the 80s," Buonorotti said.

"I bet you could still do it," she said, her eyes flaring.

"Listen, Jiggly," I said. "I hate to be the bearer of bad news, but the cops think Bowdoin is actually dead. They have a body."

This seemed to throw a switch in her.

"That fat dipstick isn't dead!"

"How do you know?"

"I know because there's a ridiculous amount of gambling going on in this tournament, and Bowdoin wouldn't miss this sort of thing if an atomic bomb landed right on him!"

"So, actually, you have no idea if Bowdoin is alive or dead?"

"Don't worry about it," she snorted. "If there's this much action in town, he'd come back to life!"

"They have a body, Jiggly. They're gonna do DNA testing to figure out exactly who it is."

"DNA testing," she snorted again. We did at least have expressive snorting in common, though her's involve a lot of shoulder action.

"And they claim he had an anchor tattoo!"

"He does have an anchor tattoo!"

"Well, he's getting deader by the minute!"

"Don't you worry! He'll show up. I'll just keep twerking around with you or one of these countless PGA guys. They're all over the place, and they're all over me. That'll bring Bowdoin out of the woodwork. He's probably following me right now!"

"Jiggly, those PGA guys already have wives and mistresses and everything."

"Yeah? Well, not a problem. And anyway, baby," she said. Now she looked me up and down like a tasty dessert. "There's always *you*."

"Ooof!" I answered. Somehow she'd grabbed my can again.

"If all hell breaks loose, and I run out of other options," she said. "They say, if you keep playing this well, you'll make the tour. Which I guess is where all the rich golfers play on TV and all that."

"That's true," I gasped, half-pretending like it might not happen. "I'd have to keep playing really well …"

Her lips quivered at me. My left knee, briefly, gave way.

"Great golf is sexy," she purred.

"I know," I purred back.

Her eyes went wild with meaning. She shot a quick look around the room, to Buonorotti, to the deputies, and back to me.

"Listen, baby," Jiggly whispered in my ear. "I gotta go now, but I'll be … around."

She took my earlobe lightly in her teeth. Her scent and body briefly traveled all over me. In a split second, time, space, gravity and arousal all raced through a kind of wormhole. Just as suddenly, I was back. She was gone, and I was aware only of the echo of clicking heels.

"Buonorotti? BUONOROTTI?!?"

"I am right here, Oose."

I caught his sleeve and held it tight.

"I can't feel my knees, Buonorotti!"

"That is very bad for the golfing, Oose."

"I mean, she's terrifying me! Which is good right? But could I be too terrified?"

"You play golf from your knees, Oose."

"Well, I gotta feel them, then, don't I?"

"The knees — and elbows — are the essence of the golf swing. This is only dimly understood."

"We gotta figure out if Bowdoin Jones is dead! If he's alive, he's the only thing that can stop Jiggly. If he's dead, me and my knees are screwed! C'mon!"

I wobble-ran out the door. Buonorotti followed.

"And where are we going, Oose?"

"To the State of Maine Morgue!"

The drive from Sennetts Harbor to Bangor was about an hour and change. A little googling along the way, with Buonorotti holding the wheel, and I had the morgue address. A little rigorous self-massaging and my knees tingled back to life.

Broadly speaking, morgue's are grim, depressing places. This one, in "downtown" Bangor, was no exception. It was in the basement of a large, square, grim, depressing, brick building.

We parked directly across the street, then did a couple laps around the building itself.

"There's electronic security at every door."

"Does this surprise you, Oose?"

"Well, I had hoped that, you know, up here in Maine, we might just be able to walk right in."

"They are more sophisticated than you expected?"

"Yeah!"

I'd led us back to a loading dock with a closed garage door. Instinctively, I felt this was our best shot. I looked it over. A high window revealed rows of fluorescent lights. I squatted down, looking for any light underneath. For ideas and angles.

"What are you going to do, Oose?"

"I don't know, Buonorotti."

A siren wailed in the distance, and at first we gave it no mind. It got closer, however. Buonorotti and I exchanged an "It can't be coming here" look, and then it appeared at the end of the block, heading our way.

The garage door started opening, and we both hopped a little.

I thought quickly.

"Wave them in!" I said and started doing so.

The truck slowed to a crawl. Then it passed us and proceeded into the garage. I experienced a nanosecond of hesitation, then saw a broad, steel step just below the truck's tailgate. I saw as well a shiny chrome handle bolted to the truck's side. I jumped up and grabbed it. I then turned to Buonorotti, waggling a finger at the matching step and handlebar on his side. He hesitated only a moment more before jumping up beside me.

We rode the truck down into a large, industrial workroom. It stopped. We stepped down and rounded the back of the truck as the driver hopped out. He looked at me, then handed me a clipboard.

I handed it back.

"Wrong guy," I said.

"Where are the right guys?"

I shrugged, then another man appeared. Tall, sloped shoulders, as pale as the full moon.

"Here he is," I said.

"Was that you with the siren?" the morgue guy asked.

"Yeah," the driver answered. "I'm in a bit of a hurry."

"Yeah, me too," the morgue guy said.

These two men each seemed to think I worked with the other one. It seemed perfectly satisfactory to all.

I pulled out my phone. I pointed to it.

"Can you guys excuse me for a second?"

They waved me away, both absorbed in the clipboard.

I walked toward a row of sheeted gurneys, inviting Buonorotti to join me.

"Use your phone," I whispered. "Pretend you're calling someone."

"I don't have a phone," he answered.

"Pretend you do," I hissed. "We're going to keep talking until these guys, who apparently both have urgent appointments, leave us alone."

"Oh. Good idea, Oose."

"Thanks! Now, pretend!"

He did. It didn't look great.

"And forget all those facial expressions!"

"What facial expressions, Oose?"

"This stuff, the pursed lips, the frowns," I said, mimicking and pointing. "Do you do that even when you're talking to someone who can't see you?"

"Pursed lips, Oose?"

I gave up.

"This is Detective Houlihan," I said loudly, then nodded at Buonorotti.

His eyes scanned the room helplessly.

"Bonjourno, Detective Houlihan," Buonorotti said, even raising an arm like a stage performance.

"Pretend you're talking to our boss!" I hissed further.

"Yes," Buonorotti said. "Yes, boss. Yes, we will."

We finally got it together, pantomiming on our phones for another five minutes. We saw the truck guy swinging into action, climbing back in and putting it in reverse. We watched the truck back out and disappear.

Another minute passed, and the morgue guy waved to us. I covered my phone, trying to look both cordial and inconvenienced.

"Can you guys lock up?" he asked, then tapped on his watch meaningfully. "You're cops, right?"

"That's right."

"Mind locking up?"

"Sure. Happy to. We're cops."

"It's just this door here," the morgue guy added. "Just need to set the lock in the knob. Like you would at home."

"Will do, buddy. Listen, I'm afraid I have to get back to this call. Big investigation."

"That's fine. Don't worry about these people," he said, throwing a thumb at the gurneys. "They're not going anywhere."

I did a big, but whisper-y laugh. He smiled brightly and gave me a thumbs-up. I returned a salute, and he disappeared.

Slowly, I lowered my phone.

"Gosh," I said. "That was easy."

I turned to Buonorotti, who looked at me, then slowly lowered his own imaginary phone. We both looked at the gurneys.

"Wanna poke a dead guy, Buonorotti?"

"Which one is it, Oose?"

We stood before the five bodies, under five sheets, on five neatly arranged gurneys.

"Well," I said, with a sigh. "There's only one way to find out."

I lifted the first sheet. An elderly woman, without an ounce of clothing, stared at the ceiling.

"Too old," I said.

The next.

"Too Chinese," I added, trying to overwhelm my dizziness with some humor.

I lifted the sheet on the fourth table, hearing a paper-y crackle and seeing little black flakes float on the air.

"This one is just right," I said.

Buonorotti took and pulled back the rest of the sheet.

"There is a tag here that reads 'B. Jones', Oose."

I followed the body to the toe tag.

"Yes …" I said.

Buonorotti caught me as I took an uneasy, half-step back.

"Do you know anything about inspecting a dead man, Oose?"

"I do," I said. "But again, only what I've read."

"On the internet?"

"Yes, Buonorotti. On the internet."

"Ah."

"This guy looks like a deep fried version of the Creature from the Black Lagoon," I observed. "How the hell would you know it's Bowdoin Jones?"

"One presumes by DNA testing," Buonorotti said.

"Right, right."

"And the policeman said he had a tattoo," Buonorotti observed. "Of an anchor. It was on his right arm."

"Yes," I said, gritting my teeth.

I did nothing.

"It would seem," Buonorotti observed. "That we cannot see all of his right arm."

"It would seem."

"Then it is but a matter of one lifting and turning the right arm. Is it not, Oose?"

This sounded like an offer. I was quick to respond.

"Would you like to do it, Buonorotti?"

"No, thank you, Oose."

"Be part of a real investigation?"

"No, though you're very kind."

"You might learn something."

"I've learned about crinkly dead people already, Oose."

"American crinkly dead people?"

"… If it's a matter of fear, Oose …"

"It's not a matter of fear!"

I extended and retracted my right hand a few times.

Finally, I pinched the scaly wrist. I felt myself grimace and the veins in my neck rise.

"Eiieeee," I slurred, then turned the arm slowly over.

We both saw a blue, spotty tattoo of an anchor. It was set in pale skin untouched by the burn.

"There it is," I observed, trying to stay cool.

"Indeed, a blue anchor tattoo," Buonorotti observed.

We both stared for a moment.

"Who the hell is this guy?"

"I do not know, Oose."

"What kind of investment banker gets an anchor tattoo?"

I raised an eyebrow at him and even was so bold as to raise the arm itself a bit higher, an instructive gesture for Buonorotti. There was, however, this kind of sticky, gooey sound. Also, the arm seemed to separate a bit from the body.

The room pixelated. My ears felt fuzzy.

I recall saying "Dang it" and then perhaps "Catch me, Buonorotti, please, gosh-dammit!" before I passed out.

CHAPTER FIVE — SATURDAY

Buonorotti somehow got us home (him to his sumptuous Victorian affair of a hotel and me to my roadside, double-decker, park-in-front, vibrating-mattress motor lodge). I'd gone directly to bed, needing my standard 8.5 hours of dreamless, pre-round rest. In all the day's drama, the reader can be forgiven for not noticing that we'd skipped both lunch and dinner. So, really, I hadn't eaten for almost 24 hours. That after 18 holes on foot, some time in jail, and the stress of breaking into a state facility brimming over with dead people. Add to that the murder charge hanging over me and the prowling sexual tigress, Jiggly Jones, out there somewhere, and I was probably burning calories faster than a marathoner on PCP.

Needless to say, the next morning I hit the players' breakfast buffet like a hurricane. It was on my third visit to the waffle station that I was blocked in my progress thereto by one Cocky Brill. This time, he was accompanied by an associate: fish-faced and English in the same fashion as Cocky, though squatter, tanner, and shave-topped.

"Oy!" Cocky began, poking a finger. "Where's your caddy, then? What, what? What?"

"He's around here somewhere, Cocky. Who's your friend?"

"My name's Barnaby Wilkes. I caddy the Euro Tour," the friend held forth, then let his eyes go googly with some kind of threat.

"Came over wif Westwood and Poulter, innit. On Poulter's jet, what? At their request. To help smarten up their gambling odds, whatsit?" Cocky said.

"Huh," I said. "I'm not tracking with some of your usage, Cocky. However, I couldn't possibly care less."

"Which is to say," Cocky continued. "That Barnaby knows everything about everything. Which is to further say he's going to figure out just who your caddy is mate!"

"I thought you took Buonorotti's picture, Cocky? Didn't that work out?"

"Well," and here Cocky blinked both eyes. "I accidentally deleted it."

"I see. Happens to the best of us. Perhaps it's just as well."

"It's just as well, alright, because Barnaby is who I would have sent the picture to anyway. Right? And this tosser was already on the plane over here, anyway. Innit? What!"

"Innit, indeed. Personally, I don't think Buonorotti's that hard to figure out, Cocky. Pro Euro-looper. Former underwear model. French Legionnaire for a couple years. Mafioso. Studied briefly for the priesthood. Jailed, again briefly, on Devil's Island. For a time he was a kind of regional superhero in Calabria, I believe."

"Right, mate, you can buy all that, but the smart money can't. We're going to find 'im out, we are!"

"Well, Cocky, Barnaby, I wish you the best of luck. Oh and by the way, what's the gambling book on me looking like?"

Despite our ongoing contretemps, Cocky and I can speak frankly about golf gambling. This is likely because he knows I hate it, so he's prepared to unload as much detail as possible.

"There's so much money riding on you, mate, it'd make your nose bleed. And every daily loser keeps pressin', dudden-he? There's one bet I heard of between a couple Aussie tour guys I won't name but whose names rhyme Mason Ray and Radam Trott that bet is currently at $1 million. US. And is entirely limited to your irons play."

"Hmm. Yes. Is Paddington here?"

"No one knows for sure, what? There is a party laying wagers under the pseudonym 'the San Diego Superchicken' which seems bloody obvious."

"Too obvious. Have you seen him anywhere?"

"I have not. I have not heard of anyone who has seen him, which makes me all the more certain he's actually here. They're all bloody here. All the Yanks. All the Euros," Cocky said. "It's like the Davis Cup of Golf Gambling!"

"We're gonna cram it up your wee gamble ginky!"

"Right! Ets go, Barnaby! Enough of this tosser fair. We're gonna find and identify your caddy, Owens!"

And with that, they were off, a bit like a Laurel and Hardy pairing, but in tropical golf colors.

It wasn't much after their departure that a violet light filled the room. A few beats later, the china shook with the sound of thunder.

"The weather looks quite threatening, Oose," Buonorotti said, appearing at my side.

"Indeed it does," I answered, just as a fissure of pink lightning connected sky to earth.

"Did Cocky track you down, Buonorotti? He remains keenly interested in your mysterious past."

"I did see him and a friend, Oose, but I avoided them both."

A distant warning siren sounded. Some mumbling, some grumbling, some crashing plates, a bit of galloping thunder, and that seemed to be it. A tour official stepped through a door, tinked a glass with a spoon, and spoke up.

"Can I have your attention, please? Everyone? With this weather, it looks like we'll have a delay of at least a couple hours. Pay attention to your phones. We'll ping you if and when we can restart."

A bit more mumbling ensued, but with a note of levity at having been given some free time. Action near the bar took on more intensity.

"Buonorotti," I said, considering the change of circumstances. "Against my better instincts, I think we need to take advantage of this delay. I think we need to do more investigating."

"Where do you propose we start, Oose?"

"Well, I think we have to presume that Bowdoin Jones is dead. Inasmuch as we've seen his body. Which was dead, as I'm sure you'll concur."

"Quite true."

"You don't get more dead than that."

"Not in my experience, Oose."

"And I've noticed that my keen PI instincts have entirely ceased spitting out new ideas."

"Is that good, Oose?"

"Not anymore."

"So what do we do?"

"I think we check out the crime scene, Buonorotti."

We took the road that followed one of the ridges, then bent around the bottom of Sennetts Harbor to drop into the parking lot. We put the Fury under a tree. I grabbed an eight iron for protection, and we marched down to the pier.

Above the harbor, electricity flickered in a dark sky, though there was no rain as of yet. Out among the clusters of boats, an array of bright orange buoys surrounded the wreckage of the Flustered Lush.

"The problem that presents itself, Buonorotti," I explained. "Is how to get out to the crime scene."

"Very true, Oose."

"And after that," I said, peering in a direction I hoped was due south. "We're not done. We want to have a look at where that body was found."

"The secondary crime scene, Oose?"

"The secondary crime scene at Newcomb's Head. Exactly right, Buonorotti."

I looked around the pier now. There were a few unattended rowboats.

"Rowboats," I observed. "No, thanks."

I walked up a bit further.

"Ah, here we are," I said, finding a dingy with a small motor. "We had a little boat very much like this when I was a boy, Buonorotti. Do you know what we called it?"

"Do tell me, Oose."

"The 'Put-Put Boat.'"

"Very good, Oose. De put-put boat."

I nodded. Looked around again, then clapped my hands. A final pause and look-about, then I lowered myself into the boat.

"We steal de put-put boat, Oose?"

"Steal?" I said, noting his hesitation and reacting quickly. "Oh, Buonorotti. Hardly. One does this sort of thing in a seaside town. You borrow one another's boats."

"Borrow?"

"Sure, like, like …" I searched here, but only for a moment. "Like umbrellas."

"Umbrellas?"

"Umbrellas," I said, smiling. "In England."

"Umbrellas in England, Oose?"

"In England," I said. "Because it rains so often, people borrow one another's umbrellas all the time."

"Without asking?"

"Exactly," I invited him in. "Without asking, you take other people's umbrellas in England. Please. Hop in."

"I grew up in a seaside town, Oose. If you borrowed someone else's boat, the owner could legally slit your throat."

"Well, that's Italy, Buonorotti," I said. "Southern Europe. Vendetta culture."

He hesitated still.

"In the English-speaking world, Buonorotti, it's all about the rule of law. And the friendly borrowing of things like boats and umbrellas."

"Are you sure, Oose?"

"Oh, quite," I said. "Really, you want people to borrow your boat. It improves your status in local, seaside society."

He hesitated a moment more, then stepped in. He looked at me, still suspicious.

"Very good," I said, yanking the cord to fire up the motor, which started immediately.

I scanned the pier and parking lot once more. Satisfied, I put it in Forward and cranked the handle.

"Here we go!" I called.

The wreckage was perhaps a quarter mile out. The Flustered Lush was ass up in the water, as were the two other sailboats. The array of orange police buoys surrounded them all.

I took us in a slow lap around all three.

"Do you count three boats, Buonorotti?"

"I do, Oose," he answered. "But what might those other things be?"

I saw that Buonorotti pointed just beyond the keel of one of the boats. A small clutch of green and blue lobster buoys floated uneasily, somehow bound together.

"Those are lobster buoys, I believe," I said. "They float, tied to traps resting on the bottom."

"Do lobstermen set traps in the middle of the harbor?" Buonorotti asked.

"I didn't think so," I answered. "But then again, what do I know?"

I put us in neutral, and we slowed to a stop in the still water. I pulled out my phone and took a few pictures. Again, we heard the rumble of thunder, but still the rain held off.

"Maybe," I said. "Bowdoin Jones had a lobstering license?"

Buonorotti said nothing, looking around.

I took us to the other side, taking more pictures.

"Both those boats look big," I said. "Sailboats, I think. This one is at least 30 feet, the other might be more."

"I think it is more, Oose," Buonorotti said. "Big boats."

"Big, expensive boats," I added. "In a little, expensive harbor."

He looked at me.

"What do you think, Oose?"

"Well," I answered. "As our bartender observed, every sailor wants to blow up his boat."

"And yet," Buonorotti answered. "How many do? It would take some nerve to do so, I think."

"Or desperation," I countered. "People do lots of nervy things when they need money."

"A keen observation, Oose."

"So that must be Newcomb's Head," and here I pointed toward an obvious jut of head-like land. "One would presume Newcomb's Neck is over in that direction."

"The body was carried out with the tide, it seems," Buonorotti observed. "Can we take this boat way out there?"

"Of course," I answered, did a furtive 320 degree scan, then cranked it.

Newcomb's Head was half a mile out. Helpfully, another smaller array of orange police buoys appeared. They surrounded three more lobster buoys.

"These buoys are green and blue," I pointed out. "Just like the others near the Flustered Lush, Buonorotti."

"Does that mean something, Oose?"

"Maybe. Maybe not. I presume you put your lobster traps in a number of places. Though it does seem strange that they're so close to both where the boats blew up and where the body was found."

I killed the engine. I looked back, as did Buonorotti.

"So the Flustered Lush blows up," I recounted, hypothetically. "Blows that fat ass-scratcher Bowdoin Jones high into the air, killing him somewhere along the way, if not instantly, and he floats out here on the tide and gets his fat, tattooed can caught up in these lobster traps. Does that all make sense?"

"I think it could make some sense, Oose."

"Me, too. Maybe these buoys are here, too, because Bowdoin came back down and got his fat, charcoaled-self tangled up in them."

"That makes sense, too," Buonorotti said. "Very sad, Oose."

"Yes," I sighed. "Every part of him sadly burnt to a crisp except his tattooed forearm."

We both sat still for a moment, listening to the ocean and the ding of a distant bell.

"Do investment guys really get anchor tattoos?" I asked, optimistically.

"I would not know that," Buonorotti answered, then paused at a memory.

"What?"

"Well," he said, then looked philosophically out to sea. "It would seem everyone gets tattoos now. I knew a nun with a tattoo."

When he didn't continue, I made him.

"Of what."

"A little scorpion," Buonorotti said, still philosophical.

"On her thigh," I whispered.

"No," Buonorotti answered, after a heavy sigh.

"Close?"

"Yes."

"Wow!"

He squinted into the wind.

"Sister Natasha."

Unintentionally, I gave the motor a little rev, and we both lunged forward, then rocked back. Fortunately, this cleared my head.

"You're right," I said. "Everyone has tattoos. Some investment douchebag is entirely likely to have an anchor tattoo, all the more so if he sails."

"And this one did," Buonorotti added.

"So where do you learn how to blow up a boat? The internet, right? But where do you get the stuff to do it?"

One of the buoys floated within reach.

"Do you use explosives in lobstering, Buonorotti?"

"I do not think so, Oose."

I reached out for the buoy and inspected it. There was no name, code or number. I thought.

"But you might have access to some crazy, explosive stuff, right?" I mused. "I mean, from some fishing/lobstering/nautical-demolition types."

"Perhaps, Oose."

"Let's see if we can find out who owns this buoy, Buonorotti."

It clipped off easily. I threw it in the boat.

"Do you think you should take that buoy, Oose? It may be connected to the trap."

"I'm sure it was. Once we find the owner, he can reattach it later."

"But the traps, Oose, are what they use to catch the lobster and make the money. You don't think it will upset this owner?"

"On the contrary, Buonorotti. We're using it to solve a crime. We'll find its owner, ask him some questions, even as we return the buoy to him at that very moment. I don't doubt that he'll be moved, morally and emotionally, by the opportunity to aid in the cause of justice. We shouldn't doubt the fundamental decency of our fellow man, Buonorotti."

"No. You are right, Oose."

"And I can't figure out how to reattach it anyway."

"You are just borrowing the buoy, then? Like an umbrella in England."

"Precisely, Buonorotti," I said. "Like an umbrella in England. Lobstermen probably want their buoys borrowed, especially under circumstances such as these."

I turned us around and gunned it back. The engine roared, but we moved maddeningly slow. As we approached the pier, the air grew warmer, and then the sun pushed out of the clouds.

"We must return and play golf, Oose," Buonorotti said, sniffing the air. "I am sure the tournament will soon resume."

"Amen, Buonorotti," I said, feeling the energy of competition surge inside me. At the same time, my phone buzzed; a text from the tour officials ordered us back for a noon restart.

"And what exactly will we do with the buoy, Oose?"

"Well, after I bang out a filthy 55, we'll drag that buoy into the local lobsterperson's bar and see if we can figure out who it belongs to."

I saw myself smile magnificently in Buonorotti's glasses.

When he said nothing, I continued.

"No doubt these lobsterpeople will be thrilled to see us and eager to help!"

Returning to the course, we found all the ingredients of a summer day set free from a bit of rough weather: a furious sun, birdsong of orchestral complexity, tawny sea breezes, bedewed flowers, glittering greens, cackling club types, carts whizzing too and fro, the crashing of surf, etc.

I came out of the gates like Secretariat, galloping over the first few holes. I'll pick up the narrative in the tee box on the fifth.

"A fade here, I think, Ooze," Buonorotti said, looking into the distance with his brooding movie idol profile. "A slight one."

I followed his gaze out into the fairway, a shimmering carpet of light. After a mystical waggle, I took two long strides to the ball, reeled back and smashed it — again without a practice swing and almost mid-stride. A 200-yard fade with a 20-yard roll.

I held my pose.

"It is exactly the fade you needed to hit, Oose."

"I was going to say 'Suck on it' right after that shot, Buonorotti, but I didn't."

"Your restraint is admirable, Oose."

I de-posed. We started down the tee box.

"I also considered, 'Me so horny!'"

"It was such a shot," Buonorotti observed. "Deserving of every accolade."

I suppose I should emphasize that I was truly in the zone here, though that somehow seems inadequate. Perhaps I should say I was in a zone inside the more traditional zone. Maybe you felt like you were once in the zone. Well, pal, I was in a zone inside of that zone *inside of that zone*. See? On every green, my mind seemed glued to the hole, such that only cataclysmic forces of nature — an earthquake, an asteroid — could untune my shots from their proper fates.

On five, given the line and speed by Buonorotti, I listened rather than watch my 30-foot putt clunk in. It was an inevitability. On six, I took a snappy, skipping, gay-Bobby-Jones kind of swing, if only to test myself. Sure enough, I caught the ball flush and sent it low, precisely as I'd envisioned. It took one elegant hop off the fairway, another, then bounded like a gazelle onto the green.

By the turn, the crowd following me had swelled to perhaps a hundred people. It included the standard clubby contingent, but also tour pros, tour groupies, gambling types, and even a couple toothy, sniveling politicians. The standard demographic set for a big golf event. And they all loved me. I felt caught in a montage of smoldering tee shots, super-subtle irons, and meandering, multi-break, 40-foot putts. Just one after the other, punctuated by deafening cheers.

I was watching just such a putt on 18. It rolled off my putter, and I stood up straight to follow it. This putt was closer to 35-feet and downhill, with three breaks, but I knew Buonorotti's read was dead on. As I recall, the sun was at its apex. Temperatures lolled around an even 80 degrees. Bosomy clouds floated in a blue sky. Risqué breezes caressed my slacks. The ball fell into the hole and triggered yet another barbaric, *Give-us-Barabbas!!* roar from the crowd.

It was only after that last putt that I noticed Lunt and his policemen. Again, they waited for me beside the clubhouse and in front of their cars. Their sirens turned, but silently. Lunt even waved his chubby little fingers at me, indicating a squad car with an open door.

"Buonorotti!" I said. "The cops are here."

"You finished ten under for the day, Oose."

"I'll bet they got the DNA evidence back," I said, scanning the terrain, thinking. "They probably can't just arrest me here, now, right on the lawn of the Sennetts Harbor Club. On their biggest day ever!"

"Tomorrow, we will play more aggressively, Oose."

"Buonorotti!" I said, grabbing him. "Let's do this: get the Fury! Meet me on the far side of the clubhouse!"

"Very good, Oose."

"And keep the car running," I said. "I may be coming in hot!"

We exchanged these last words as we walked through a seething crowd to the scorer's trailer. Buonorotti peeled off. A few paces ahead, Lunt awaited me.

"Another exciting development in the case, Lieutenant?"

"That's right, Owens. We'd like to talk to you again."

"I'd love to help. Mind if I turn in my scorecard first? Then I'll meet you right here?"

"Sure," he said, as I stepped inside the trailer.

I closed the door, then seized the first local type I found.

"Where do working lobsterpeople hang out around here?"

"Beal's," he answered.

"And where's that?"

"By the hah-bah."

"The hah-bah?"

"Ayuh. It's a bah."

"Itzabah?"

"Ayuh. At the hah-bah. Right by."

"Right by what?"

"The hah-bah."

"Itzabah?"

"Ayuh."

"Beal's?"

"Right by."

We did a couple laps of this Abbott and Costello routine, but I eventually figured out that Beal's was a bar in town by the harbor.

"Great!" I said.

"Ayuh," he answered.

I went through the remaining rigamarole with the officials. That settled, I proceeded to the backdoor. Like any residence, a trailer must have multiple entry and exit points. This was about a three-quarter-length trailer with a back door at the far end. I just walked right on, looking through what windows I could as I progressed. I pulled back a cotton shade on the back door. There were no cops and only a few people, all turned the other direction. Fifty yards ahead, I saw Buonorotti roll up in the Fury, stop and swing his mirrors my way.

I took a deep breath, opened the door, and stepped down.

"Hey," a kid in a bucket hat said. "It's Owens! Great round, Owens!"

I nodded, gave him a thumbs-up, and started running like heck for the Fury, a chorus of "Heys!" and "Owens!" and "Stop him!" and "Police!" behind me.

I leapt over the door and into the passenger seat like one of the Duke boys.

"Step on it, Buonorotti!"

He didn't have to be told. We sprayed grass and grit everywhere as Buonorotti peeled an s-skid toward the road. I clapped my hat on top of my head, then checked the backseat: the buoy was still there, hopping around on the vinyl.

"Where shall we go, Oose?"

"Beal's, Buonorotti!"

"Where is that, Oose?"

"Itzabah by the hah bah!"

Beals, as it turned out, was equal parts dive bar and working lobster pier. It was also well populated with working lobsterpeople, all huddled around a bar improvised from multi-colored lobster traps. The men appeared as one would expect, deeply browned by the sun, crows feet at the corners of the eyes, scruffy beards, baseball caps, knurled hands, various other knurled features. There seemed to be little conversation, and what little there was seemed low and grim.

"Oose, if I may," this was Buonorotti talking, and he was standing beside me. "I would not say that you borrowed that buoy as you did. My sense is that it would not be well-received."

"Hmm?" I answered, then made the connection. "Ah, right. Some bad attitudes in here, you're saying. Good idea. I'll say I found it."

"That would be better, Oose."

"Right," I said. "Well, looks like it's time for the old Charm Offensive, Buonorotti."

I cranked my smile up to eleven, then held up the buoy.

"Heyooo!" I said, announcing myself. The *Heyoo*, as some of the other pro jocks call it, is this sort of sing-song-y, Ed-McMahon thing I do. The guys generally love it, and it seemed like just the right introductory note to strike here.

And of course, under normal circumstances, it would have been. These were, however, rustic, hardworking, hard-bitten types. The sea, as I believe Nelson said, is a cruel taskmaster. Perhaps, additionally, they were sensitive to fate, as they all seemed to turn and immediately focus on my outfit. Here I was in my pink shirt (with dazzles), white belt (also with dazzles), white shoes (no dazzles) and savage tan (apart from my forehead). There they were, with their aforementioned crow's feet, cigarettes, snarls, gnarls, and various knurled parts, none of which featured any dazzles at all.

I stopped myself. I am, unfortunately, a bit prone to over-analysis. Perhaps the Heyoo had no real effect. Perhaps, in fact, these men — and one woman, every bit as salty and knurled as the rest — were too fixated on the buoy in my hand to see anything else. Many seemed to be.

I decided I had no choice but to lean into it. I held the buoy high.

"Fellas," I said. "Forgive me, but I'm hoping to find the owner of this buoy. I was led to believe I might find him here, and I'd like to return it. It's important to emphasize that I found it. This buoy, that is."

"Where'd you find it?" one of them asked. He had a rich, greasy, blonde beard and a significant jaw that was mostly on the left-hand side of his head. Like Popeye.

"By Newcomb's Head," I answered.

There was a bump of dead air, which I felt compelled to fill.

"Just past Newcomb's Neck," I added.

Popeye's sidekick, who was roughly three times Popeye's size but with a jet black beard, swung his stool fully to me. And Popeye wasn't small, I should note.

"You're not supposed to have that," Blackbeard said. "Another man's buoy. That's a man's living."

"You ain't, in fact, supposed to even touch another man's buoy," Popeye said.

"Ayuh," Blackbeard contributed.

"Ayuh," I said, working the vernacular. "Well, I *found* it, as I said, and be that as it may, do you know whose buoy it is?"

"We do."

I looked at Buonorotti.

"Great," I said. "Do you have a name?"

"Sure," Blackbeard answered. "But why don't you just leave it with us."

"Isn't the owner here?"

"He's a bit of a recluse," Popeye answered.

"I see. And his name is ..."

"We don't share things like that, as I said," Blackbeard answered.

"I just want a name, fellas," I said, looking around. "I'm trying to figure out what happened on that boat that blew up."

"Why?"

"Well, as it happens, I'm accused of blowing up that boat."

"You're accused of arson, then?" Blackbeard asked. "And murder, if I've heard right."

"That's right. Which is why I need the name of the guy who owns this buoy."

"To take the fall for you, you're saying?" Popeye contributed.

I'd clearly made a tactical misstep here.

"Yes. Right. What? NO!"

Also, I noticed a heightening of the hostility in the room, which was already pretty heightened. I made a quick decision and whipped out my PI's badge.

"Alright. I didn't want to do this, but my name's U.S. Owens. Detective U.S. Owens," I said, significantly. "I'd like that name please. Now."

Blackbeard took a long careful look at the badge. He was perhaps ten feet away.

"You're a cop?"

"I am," I said. "And this is important cop business. So kindly give me that name before me and my deputy here have to take you downtown."

"Downtown," Blackbeard enquired, with a glance at Popeye.

"Downtown," I said. "*Bangor town.*"

It was a bad addition, which I knew even as I said it, but was powerless to stop. In any event, it didn't affect Blackbeard. He took another glance at the badge, then his big black eyes, suddenly quite bright and smart, tangled up with mine.

"That's a private investigator's license," he observed.

"No," I parried. "It's not."

"I can read it."

"You can?"

"Yeah."

"From all the way over there?"

"Yeah," he said. "And it was hard to reconcile with your overall appearance. Unless, of course, you're undercover."

There was laughter, here. Blackbeard stood with a smile.

"You've got a shifty way about you that I don't like," he said. "Let's step outside."

"What?!"

Popeye stood now, too.

"You can leave the buoy and run," Popeye suggested. "If you'd prefer that."

"What is this? Hardcastle and McMcCormick?!"

No one got that reference.

"Is this some bad TV show?" I continued, "'Step outside'?"

"We'll step outside and talk, friend," Blackbeard added.

"Can you believe this, Buonorotti?'"

"I cannot believe this," Buonorotti answered.

"I can't believe it either. You guys are really freaking out about a styrofoam buoy!"

Neither answered this time.

"So you're through talking?" I said, shaking my head.

They apparently were.

"Fine!" I continued, after a pause. "Let's step outside and fight!"

I held up a hand, inviting Blackbeard and Popeye to lead the way.

"After you," I said. "Let's all of us just step outside. Show us where you want this big fight to go down!"

They did so, and when both lobstermen passed us, I ran like heck for the kitchen.

"C'mon, Buonorotti!" I called over my shoulder.

I'd already blazed through the swinging door, smashed through the back, and taken cover behind some cars. From here I hoped to wave in Buonorotti without overexposing myself, so to speak.

He didn't appear.

"Buonorotti?" I called.

I waited two minutes. Then five.

Then Buonorotti stepped out of the back door and looked around. There wasn't a mark on him.

"Oose?" he said. "Are you nearby, Oose?"

"I'm over here, Buonorotti! Come quick!"

I rose just enough for him to see me. I waved aggressively.

"Is okay, Oose," he said. "I took care of the matter. Come inside, please."

"You took care of it?"

"Yes," he said, with a flex of the lips. "Is taken care of."

I stood, reluctantly, and in stages. He waved me forward.

"You mean, you took care of those two huge lobstermen?"

"Yes, Oose," he answered. "I stepped outside with them. I tried to explain to them that I had been a professional fighter and killed men and bada beep bada boop bada beep they want to fight anyway and I won."

I stood up entirely.

"Oh," I said.

"Come," he answered, holding the door.

I entered. Everyone stared at us like we'd just arrived from outer space. We passed through the front door to find Popeye and Blackbeard splayed flat on the asphalt, both out cold.

"You *were* in the Foreign Legion, Buonorotti!"

"Is true."

"Of course, I would have, you know, stayed and fought, too — "

"I have no doubt, Oose."

" — but I can't afford to damage my hands or really even any part of my body. Because of the tournament."

"It was smart of you to remove yourself so efficiently, Oose."

"I thought so! Anyhow, nice work," I said, then thought. "Did they tell you the name of the lobsterman who owns that buoy?"

"His name is Mike Lunt, Oose," Buonorotti said.

"Jeez! Is everyone here named Lunt!"

"A great many people, Oose."

"Did they say where Mike Lunt lives?"

"He lives on Singer's Island, Oose."

"And how do we get there?"

"I was informed, Oose, that we take the ferry at the end of this road. That takes us to Swan's Island."

"But you said Singer's Island?"

"Yes. As I was told, once on Swan's Island, we 'find a guy' to take us to Singer's Island. It is a much smaller island."

"I guess there's a lot of islands around here."

"So it would seem, Oose."

"The plot thickens, Buonorotti!"

With Buonorotti behind the wheel, we roared down a two-lane street, passing the occasional house, usually fronted by an arrangement of buoys, uncut grass and the obligatory boat-on-blocks. The ferry came into view around a bend. It was blowing its whistle, ready to depart. We parked the Fury and barely scrambled aboard in time.

We set forth into a bank of fog a couple hundred yards out on the ocean. After half an hour, Swan's Island emerged from the void. On the pier, we found a guy in coveralls willing to motor us out to Singer's Island.

"Who lives out on Singer's Island?" I asked as we left.

"Just the Lunt's," the guy said.

"Which ones?"

"The crazy ones, mostly."

"How many crazy ones are on this particular island?"

"A lot," he said.

"Can you name any of them?"

"Mike Lunt," he answered. "A few of his brothers."

"What are their names?"

"I don't remember, exactly," he said. "They all answer to 'Mike,' though."

"Ah," I said.

"Or 'Lunt,'" he added.

"Sure," I said.

Buonorotti raised another eyebrow at me.

Singer's Island materialized from the fog, then a short metal pier.

"Just follow the shore road clockwise," the guy said, roping us up. "The camps start maybe half a mile that way."

"Great," I answered. "And you'll stay here?"

"As long as you're paying me," he said.

We got out. My spikes rang out against the steel.

After a ten minute walk along the shore road — little more than a pair of wheel ruts through the pines — a two-story, cedar-shingled cottage came into view. A swing set rusted in a corner. Half a lobster boat floated in the grass behind it. On the walls were the requisite buoys.

"Those buoy colors match the one I found, Buonorotti."

"The one you borrowed, Oose, for the investigation."

"That's right, Buonorotti."

I stopped us. I lifted a hand to the side of my face.

"Hello!" I called, not unlike a Switzer yodeling over the Alps.

We heard nothing but the sea crashing on the nearby rocks.

We took a few steps closer.

"Mike!?" I called out this time, just as loud, but with more optimism that he wasn't actually around.

No one answered.

I found a screen door and pulled it open.

"Mike?" I said. "Mikey? It's me! Lunt!"

Satisfied there was no one home, I stepped inside. The living room was a junkyard of beer cans and pizza boxes, phone books and fishing magazines.

I took a step through a door and into the kitchen, and there it all was: everything you'd need to make a bomb, carefully laid out on the table — at least what I'd imagine was everything. Wires, fuses, clocks. Sagging in a chair like a kid waiting for dinner was a 50lb bag of fertilizer.

"Buonorotti!?" I called, excitedly.

He joined me, immediately focusing on the table.

"Oose," he said. "This looks like some kind of dangerous project."

"Yeah!" I said, getting even more nervous. "A boat bomb project!"

"You think that plastic jug is ammonia, Oose?"

"Do you use ammonia in explosives!?"

"Yes, Oose."

"Then I think that's what it is!"

I'm using all these exclamation points to emphasize that I was fairly excited.

"I'm not used to being around explosives, Buonorotti!"

"It is normal to be nervous, Oose."

"You've been around a lot of explosives?! In the Foreign Legion?!"

"Well, I was around the explosives like this with some of the girls from the convent. After we had left the convent, of course. I taught Latin at a convent in Andorra."

I turned to him. He saw I needed more.

"These young girls had fallen from the faith, Oose."

"I'll say!"

"I confess that I had fallen from the faith as well," he added. "We lived in a kind of sin."

"With these terrorist ex-nuns! You mean there was a lot of ..."

"Of the bada-boop-ing, yes, Oose. They were relentless in the badabooping."

"Jiminy Christmas!!!"

"And uncompromising in their politics."

"That's less interesting!"

"They never took off their bandoleros ..."

"Even during the ...?"

"Even during the badabooping, yes, Oose. It was a troubling time."

I was dizzy for a moment.

"Alright, ALRIGHT!" I said, forcing myself back on track. "Let's focus on the case, Buonorotti!"

"Yes, Oose."

I turned back to the table.

"You think these are detonators?!" I asked, pointing at some things that looked like boxy, slightly oversized nine-volt batteries.

"I ..."

I didn't let him finish.

"Jock Freaking Ewing! These are detonators! There's a box with a picture of these things! The box says 'Detonators', Buonorotti!"

"Well ..." Buonorotti said.

"Well?!"

He refocused on the table and gave a mysterious squint.

"Why are you squinting again?"

"Squeenting?"

"When you narrow your eyes like that? That's squinting!"

"Squeenting," he said. "It's a funny word. I did not know it. Squeenting."

"Yeah, squeenting! Why are you doing that?"

"No reason, Oose."

"Squinting!" I said, a bit freaked out. "At a time like this! With bomb stuff all over the place!"

"I'm sorry, Oose. I won't … squeent."

"I'm calling Lunt!" I said, taking out my phone.

"Owens," Lunt answered.

"Listen to me, Lunt!" I said. "I'm out on Singer's Island in the home of the guy who blew up the Flustered Lush! I'm staring at a kitchen table full of explosives!"

"Sure, you are," he said. "Listen, Owens. There's a warrant out for your arrest. You need to turn yourself in."

"You weren't going to investigate this angle, Lunt, so I had to!" I answered. "I'll take a picture and send it to you!"

"Whatever," he answered.

"Yeah, whatever is right!" I said. "Whatever you need to make a bomb! Which is what is here! Let me put you on speaker!"

I pulled the phone down to take my picture. I was framing it up. The light was terrible.

"Trace this call!" I barked at Lunt. "If you want to come out and see what's going on!"

"Oh, we will," he answered. "And why don't you just stay right there, Owens. You and your butt buddy, Buonoriggi."

"It's all here, Lunt!" I sneered. "Fertilizer! Fuses! Clocks! You could blow up all the boats in Sennetts Harbor with what he's got here, Lunt!"

"Why are you yelling, Owens?"

"Because I'm freaking out, Lunt! Surrounded as I am by freaking explosives! Now shut up and let me take these pictures!"

With Lunt on speaker, I framed up the shot, pulling back get in the ammonia, detonators, and sack of nitrates. The phone pushed and zoomed trying to bring everything into focus.

"What are you doing, Owens?"

"I'm taking a picture of this bomb stuff, Lunt! It just won't come into focus!"

"Is that an iPhone?"

"Yeah!"

"Put us on FaceTime!"

"How?!"

"There's a little thing in the corner, Owens. Tap that."

"What does it look like, Lunt?! There's little things all over this thing!"

"Dammit, Owens, it's like a rectangle!"

And I would have barked back. Instead, I leapt high into the air, prompted to do so by an enormous explosive sound from the front yard.

"What was that?" Lunt asked from my phone.

"It's the Lobsterman Mike Lunt," Buonorotti announced, peering around a curtain. "And he has a shotgun, Ooze."

"Get the hell out of my house!" the nearer Lunt shouted, without.

"You hear that, Lunt!?!" I said into the speakerphone. "It's your lobsterman cousin, Mike!! The guy you should be looking for! He's shooting at us!!!"

I joined Buonorotti at the window to watch Lobsterman Lunt fire another load of buckshot in the air.

"What?" Lieutenant Lunt said. "I can't tell what's going on, Owens, with all that noise! Who are you talking to?"

"Thieves!!" Lobsterman Lunt cried. "Get out!!"

And so we did, prompted by a load of buckshot through the other kitchen window. Prudently, we ran for the opposite side, out the house's screened front door, and across the lawn

"Were those the fireworks?" Lieutenant Lunt asked from the phone in my hand.

"Those were shotgun blasts, Lunt!"

Lobsterman Lunt shot again. At us. Or rather just ever so slightly above our heads.

"LUNT!!" I said, trying to point the phone back toward Lobsterman Lunt.

"What?!"

"LOOK!!"

"We're not on Facetime, Owens!"

"AREN'T WE?!" I answered. "HE'S SHOOTING AT US!"

"Who is?"

"YOUR COUSIN!"

"Who?"

"LUNT!"

"Yeah?!"

"NO!"

"WHAT?!"

Lieutenant Lunt started to say something about leaving the premises, but I missed it — I'd dropped the phone in the grass.

"DANG!!" I said, turning around for it.

"What are you doing, Oose?"

"I dropped my phone!" I said, hunting around in the weeds.

"I think it would be best if you left it behind, Oose."

"It's my phone, Buonorotti!"

Lobsterman Lunt fired again. A bucketful of dirt rose into the air about ten feet away from me, and I decided I could in fact leave the phone behind.

"Owens?!" I heard from somewhere in the grass. "Is that gunfire?"

"Yes!" I called back to it as I ran. "It is gunfire, Lunt!"

"I'll advise you to take shelter," he said.

"Thanks!" I answered, over my shoulder. "BUTTHOLE!!"

Lobsterman Lunt fired again, and tree material showered us as we sprinted through the woods.

"Was that lunatic shooting at you?" the boat-hand laughed, shaking his head.

"He was!!" I cried, following Buonorotti into the boat and waving the boathand in. He did get in, very leisurely.

"He does that to everybody," the boathand chuckled, firing up the engine and taking a fast, wide arc out into the ocean.

We hid behind a few pine trees while the Swans Island Ferry unloaded. When no policemen of any variety appeared, we ran like hell for the gangplank and boarded.

It was the 4:30 ferry. The last one. And it was just Buonorotti, me and a couple vacationing families-of-four.

With a forty minute ride back, I calmed down enough to describe out loud how I saw the case.

"So this Jiggly, the sparkly blonde little tramp, hires me at the club bar to find her philandering husband," I began. "That's how we start the case. Having incapacitated Auchincloss Hastings Burr, I'm screwed. With no hope remaining to even break 80 the next day, I take the job."

"I feel we will play extraordinary golf tomorrow, Oose," Buonorotti observed. "As frightened as you now are."

"I had been drinking that night," I conceded. "Nevertheless, I find her husband, Bowdoin Jones, at the Sennetts Harbor pier, where he attacks me, demands that I stay away from his wife, then takes off in his dingy."

Buonorotti: "It will be a perfect day, I think. The humidity will be negligible. It will be dry all night. The course will be quite quick."

"In the morning, the boat blows up," I continue. "It's soon apparent I've been framed by both Joneses for the murder of husband Bowdoin Jones. After which, so terrorized, I play a masterful first round, now confident I'm again in grave danger. The local cop, Lunt, assures me I'm a lead suspect in this boat explosion/missing persons case."

"You have played magnificently, Oose," Buonorotti said, his attention returning from the sea. "And you have played more quietly each day."

"Jiggly Jones reappears, even tartier than before," I say, allowing myself a moment with this memory. "She explains that it's all some kind of scheme to free her husband from a bad investment swindle. You and I had meanwhile learn that two other boats blew up. I, in my shortsighted way, tell her this. I tell her as well that there's millions of dollars riding on this tournament. She gets angry. She's convinced Bowdoin's playing gambling and arson angles he never told her about. She's not gonna let him keep that money from her."

"The more quiet your game, Oose," Buonorotti said. "The more brilliant it becomes."

"Perhaps," I say, straightening up. "Be that as it may, an actual dead body arrives stage right."

"This morning, with this crazy woman after you and a new dead body, you played as well as anyone in the world, Oose."

"You and I inspect said dead body ourselves. It is, by all appearances, Bowdoin Jones, charred to a seaweedy crisp," I thought a bit more. "Of course, Jiggly is convinced he's still very much alive."

"On 17, considering the low barometric pressure I anticipate tomorrow, I'd like you to play the 3-iron fade off the tee, Oose."

"We get arrested. Jiggly springs us, announcing that she will continue to wear skimpy attire in an effort to provoke Bowdoin's jealousy and draw him out. Perhaps even bring him back from the dead. I think she could do it! In any event, you and I start investigating in earnest. We match the buoy to Mike Lunt back there on Singer's Island where we find a boatload, if you'll pardon the expression, of material for homemade explosives."

"And on six. It is a similar dogleg right. If it is as dry as we expect, we can play a long run."

"So, Mike Lunt would be our perp. The guy who helped Bowdoin Jones blow up his own and three other boats. Would he not?"

"Hmm?"

"I think Bowdoin Jones hired Mike Lunt to blow up his boat and fake his death."

"Oh, yes, Oose. Remember you will fade a three-iron low on six and seventeen."

"But then who's the dead guy, if it's not Bowdoin Jones?"

"Yes, Oose …" Buonorotti said, making notes in his book.

"And if it's not Bowdoin Jones, how do you produce an additional dead guy so fast?"

"Another good question."

"Are you even paying attention, Buonorotti?"

"I am not."

I considered this, allowing myself the briefest flicker of indignation.

"Do you only think of golf, Buonorotti?"

"I only think of golf, that is right."

"There are bigger deals," I said. "In life …"

"I do not think so, Oose."

"Sure, there are."

He looked up from his book.

"Tell me about them, Oose."

"Well, if we don't figure this stuff out, we're both going to jail. Jail is a big deal."

"Okay, Oose," he said. He thought. "Who is this person who is dead who we saw, if it is not the husband, Bowdoin Jones?"

"That's the question, isn't it? Maybe it's another lobsterman. Just another dead guy who they've swapped in for Bowdoin Jones?"

"But didn't the policeman think he could match the body with the DNA?"

"Which I think they've probably done. Which is why they wanted to arrest us again earlier today ..."

"But you still don't think it's him?"

"I don't. Because Jiggly doesn't. Heck, she thought he was following her around, overcome with jealousy!"

"It is quite far-fetched, Oose."

"And there's no real reason to believe her, right? I mean, everything points to Bowdoin being entirely dead!"

"Murder is a serious crime, for which you will go to a very bad jail, Oose," Buonorotti said. "Are you not concerned?"

"Sure, I'm concerned. Concerned out of my freaking gourd!"

"That concern will be very good for your golf tomorrow."

He met my narrowed eyes with his brightest smile.

"Ah, good!" Buonorotti continued, looking past me and nodding. "The policemen are waiting on the dock. They will be eager to hear your theories, Oose."

I scrambled down the ferry gangway or whatever they call it toward the little gaggle of cops and spinning sirens that awaited us.

"Lunt!" I called. "You gotta get a boat out to Singer's Island! The killer and all his bomb-making gear are right ... BLURFG!"

I ended with the "BLURFG" because that was in fact the sound that came out of my mouth. As I scampered toward Lunt, eager to get him out to the island, bagging evidence, capturing his crazy cousin and exonerating me, but he instead nodded as I approached, then threw me in an arm bar and rammed me up against a police cruiser.

"Hey?!" I said, catching my breath. "The bad guy — the perp! — is right out there! On Singer's Island?"

"Oh, yeah?"

"YEAH!"

Buonorotti was arm-barred as well and similarly thrown up against the car beside me.

"I took pictures of all his ammonia and detonators and stuff. BOMB stuff!"

"Is that right?" Lunt asked.

"You don't believe me?"

"No, I don't," he said, lifting half his mustache. "The DNA evidence came back. You're officially under arrest for the murder of Bowdoin Jones."

"But whoever actually did blow up Bowdoin Jones lives out there!"

"Is that right?"

"Yes! It is. I think the real perp is your cousin, Mike Lunt!"

"My cousin, Mike Lunt, is working at an alligator farm in Ft. Lauderdale, Florida."

"Well," I said. "Maybe he came back? There's a huge pile of evidence out there, Lunt!"

At that very moment, the sky filled with a broad, blue light, then the ground was raked with an incredible gust, and finally a huge boom rattled my eardrums like a pair of basketball-sized maracas. Helplessly, we all turned to see a modest-sized mushroom cloud appear over the ocean.

"There goes your huge pile of evidence, Owens," Lunt said.

"Well, then, clearly, the lobsterman we saw is Bowdoin Jones!"

It had come to me in a flash while we sat cuffed up in the back of Lunt's squad car. I looked at Buonorotti, who did a frown-n-shrug that seemed to mean, "Sure, that could be true!"

"It's him! It's gotta be. That's where Bowdoin's hiding out! In your cousin's seedy freaking lobster shack!!"

"Uh-huh," Lunt answered over his shoulder.

"You're not going to go back and check it all out? He had detonators and ammonia and fertilizer all over the place, Lunt?"

"All over the place being the operative phrase," Lunt answered, casually looking out the window.

"It doesn't look like you're going to! I didn't see any cops jump on the ferry before it left just now!"

"We'll take the boat. We have a police boat."

"You gotta do it right now! Before all the evidence floats away in the atmosphere. Or to the bottom of the ocean! I mean don't you have to investigate a massive explosion, at least!?"

"Don't worry about it," he said, still casually regarding the countryside.

"Don't worry about it? Don't worry about it?!"

"It is okay, Oose," Buonorotti said. "You will play even better now, because your likelihood of evading this crime has been significantly diminished and you have even more to worry about."

"Thanks, Buonorotti!"

"And we have the pictures on your phone," Lunt added.

"The phone is out on the island!" I said, somewhat exasperated. "Bowdoin was destroying all his evidence! He probably blew that up, too!"

"Or else you were," Lunt said. "You were blowing it all up and destroying all of your own evidence."

Buonorotti leaned forward.

"This man does need to play in the tournament tomorrow, officer," he said.

"Then he'll need to come up with about $200,000 cash for bail," Lunt answered.

"Bowdoin is alive and kicking somewhere, Lunt!" I said.

"Not according to the DNA and forensics lab."

"And they did their analysis overnight? That sounds pretty hasty, if you ask me!"

"Well, Owens, we're pretty efficient up here in Maine. It's our Yankee heritage."

"Oh, yeah? I got your Yankee heritage right here, Lunt!"

"Delightful," he said.

"What do you have against me, Lunt?" I said. "You got some beef with me that I just can't figure out."

He turned.

"Maybe I'm eccentric," he said, over his twitchy mustache. "But I just don't like murderers."

"I didn't murder anybody!"

"Or playboy golfers," he added.

"I'm *celibate.*"

Lunt scoured us with his eyes.

"It's true, my friend," Buonorotti added.

"You're celibate for golf," Lunt said.

"That's right."

"It is the gravest of sacrifices," Buonorotti said. "He plays much, much better. Everyone does."

"You're celibate, and yet you carried on this affair with Jiggly Jones?"

"I never met her before Wednesday night!"

"We have all that evidence. The pictures. The videos."

"That *they* gave you! *You're* the police! Do some *police work!*"

He chortled, as did the cop behind the wheel.

Buonorotti said, gesturing to me, "Are you so blind that you cannot see how powerfully attractive Oose Owens is to women? The celibacy alone drives them mad. He is at one time ugly and gorgeous, like Don Juan, Genghis Khan, Woody Allen and a thousand other sexual heroes of history."

"See!?"

"Add to that the contempt for fate, the lawlessness, and, most importantly, the monomania for the one thing in life more alluring than money, fame, enlightenment, or even sex."

"Which is?" Lunt asked.

"Golf, my friend."

"Yeah!" I said. "Golf!"

"Right."

"I can't help it if Jiggly's into me. I'm a pro golfer!"

Lunt stopped chortling instantly.

"Semi-pro," he said. "And when you go to jail and become a professional convict rather than athlete, she won't be that into you anymore, will she, Owens?"

I found myself leaning forward, trying to get a better look at Lunt. He quickly turned back.

"You know Jiggly's going to bail us out, don't you, Lunt?" I said, when he wouldn't make eye contact.

"She'll need about two hundred grand, cash," he answered.

"You don't think she can shake that out of one of these private-equity-boat-owner douchebags? To her, they're like freaking ATMs!"

"We're here," Lunt said, as we turned into the police station. "This must almost feel like home now, Owens."

We were ushered to our cell, where once again Buonorotti and I took up our positions on opposite benches.

Buonorotti, in an effort to distract me, continued recounting his tale of the former nuns with whom he'd lived in Andorra. It involved terrorism, nymphomania, dynamite and bank robbery. It was indicative of my overall state of mind that I barely listened.

The afternoon twiddled away to nothing and soon the sun set. Trapped as we were, it made the arrival of a perfect summer evening even more poignant.

"Remember, Oose. On two, I would like you to hit that stinger."

"Right."

"With a draw, please. A slight one."

"Yes."

"Are you listening, Oose?"

"I am not."

"You are worried about this murder charge."

"Yes!"

"I could see how distressed you are, Oose, and I understand. It is not merely the golf. It is this woman. Jiggly."

"She's gorgeous and insane, and she'll be here any minute!" I coughed up. "She probably did kill her husband!"

"Yes, such women do such things," he said, lifting his eyes to the cell window in thought. "They are ... insatiable."

"Yes," I said. "If by insatiable you mean freaking nuts!"

"You have played like a golfing genius for days, Oose," he said, with an abrupt solemnity. "You have quieted your game. I think, in a way, you may not need me anymore."

"What?!"

"I think you can make your own reads now, Oose."

"The last thing I need is for you to ditch me! I need you more than ever now! Jiggly's out there!"

"You told me just the other day, Oose, after that magnificent four-break, downhill putt on the fifth hole," he said. "That you intended to say something involving many lewd concepts that even I did not understand, and yet you didn't say it."

"Was it 'Reacharound ranchhand'?"

"No."

"'Snaggletaint'?"

"No."

"'Sniff my snagglefrog'?"

"Yes, that was it."

"I don't even know what those mean! I'm working entirely in abstractions! I'm that unhinged! It's like I'm speaking in tongues! I'm like the golf version of Nell out there!"

"And yet you're not speaking at all, which is the essence of it. That is your breakthrough, Oose."

"I'm speaking in tongues, but only to myself? That's my breakthrough?"

"Precisely, Oose."

"Well," I huffed. "Maybe I can quiet my game, but that doesn't mean I don't need your help on the greens! Or all over the freaking course!"

Buonorotti considered this. A tiny constellation of lightning bugs twirled in the cell window.

"Oose?"

"Yes?"

"Why do you hate gambling so?"

" … I …"

"There is no reason not to tell me. We are in jail together. For the second time. It is hard to be more intimate than this, in a decent way, in jail, and I have told you many lurid things of my past."

I inhaled briefly.

"My name is Ulysses Slayton Owens," I began. "Right?"

"Yes?"

"You know why my middle name is 'Slayton'?"

"No?"

"Because my father, the astronaut, bet Deke Slayton, the bigger and more important astronaut, that the Russians would beat us to the moon. The Russians! And when he lost, Slayton got to provide my first AND middle name, which he did. Ulysses Slayton! US! Meanwhile, NASA found out. My father was convinced it kept him from landing on the moon. He was never going to the moon! His name was Algernon Bumpus Owens. Who's going to the moon? Neil Armstrong and Buzz Aldrin? Or Algernon Bumpus?"

"I see," Buonorotti said.

"Betting on the Russians beating us to the moon! What kind of hen-dingler does that?"

"I would not know what kind hen-dinger."

"And then, when he realized his career was kaput in the Space Program, he took me on a world tour of all the US military posts around the globe. What were we doing? Allegedly we were on a NASA publicity junket. In reality, he was using me to hustle golf on every military course from Pearl Harbor to Czechoslovakia!"

"Goodness!"

"Every morning I'm hustling some full bird colonel. Or the commander of all the submarines in the Atlantic Ocean! COMSUBLANT, Buonorotti! The guy thinks he can golf, and I scalp him! Me! A buck-toothed, pimple-faced, twelve-year-old!"

"Mio dio."

"He was such a compulsive gambler, and he paid such a steep price, that he made me swear never to gamble myself."

"Yesss … I can understand your strong feelings."

"And that's why we don't gamble on US Owens's round."

He clicked his tongue.

"Have you considered the money … "

"Wait!" I interrupted. "Shhh!"

My keen hearing had picked up voices coming from the front of the station.

"It's Jiggly!"

Buonorotti raised an ear.

"Yes. Just as you thought, Oose."

"She's talking to Lunt!" I whispered.

"I don't hear him?"

"Well, she's doing most of the talking!"

Pretty soon that stopped, and we listened to the crescendo of her high heels ticking over the concrete floor.

"She's coming this way!"

I scrambled for a place to hide.

"Perhaps," Buonorotti said, observing. "I may help with this crazy beautiful woman, Oose ..."

"Save yourself, Buonorotti!"

The clickity-ticking stopped.

"Where's that deputy?" we heard Jiggly snap. "That Italian beefcake is in there with him!"

There was a scramble of rubber-soled shoes, the deputy appeared, unlocked our cell, charged in, wrapped up Buonorotti, and marched him out.

"Where's he going?" I asked.

"Next door," the deputy answered.

"Why?"

"Oose," Buonorotti said, as the deputy tugged on him. "Remember: the sexy women are bad for golf."

"I know, Buonorotti!"

With that, he was gone, and Jiggly appeared. She just walked right into the cell, set a hand on her perfect hip, and lifted her chin.

I gulped, a distant cell door clanked shut, and in the blink of bee's eye, she was on me like a wetsuit.

"Oooof!"

"Oooh, I know, Oozy, honey, I missed you, too."

I started to say something more, but she pinned my lips up with her finger.

"Hush. Shhh. Shut up," she said, then, looking over her shoulder, whispered. "We've got to be discrete."

"Disthcrete?"

"You're absolutely killing this tournament, baby."

I pried her finger from my lips.

"Jiggly! They've got DNA evidence that Bowdoin is dead!"

"He is dead," she purred.

"He is?!?"

"Or so they say," her lips gave a Marilyn-Monroe-like lip-quiver. "In any event, it means you and I can get married."

"MARRIED?"

"Shhssh …" she said. "Right after you win this tournament, baby, Oozy, honey …"

She did another Marilyn-Monroe lip twitch.

"Married?" I whimpered. "I thought you were after actual PGA Tour guys. You said they're all over the place! And all over you!"

"They are, but so are their lawyers," she sniffed. "I had to, like, legally agree to a couple non-binding, entirely inconsequential one-night stands!"

"Really?"

"Really. Every time! Totally classless, and anyway, I like you."

She closed for a kiss. Her mouth, full and sweet, pressed to mine. She pulled herself back to look at me.

"I'm celibate," I gasped.

"Ha!" she answered.

"…"

"What, really?" she said.

"Yes!"

"Why?"

"Because," I said, aware of my darting, shameful eyes. "Because I play better that way."

"You play better golf?"

"That's right."

"You're kidding."

"No!" I said. "I'm not!"

She considered me a bit longer, then seemed to decide something.

"That's cute. We'll take care of it, baby," she said, then squeezed my can again. "The old-fashioned way."

"But I'm going to jail! For killing your husband!"

She rolled her eyes and said, "That'll never happen."

"It won't?"

"Not if you win, Oozy."

"What do you mean? After the tournament, they're gonna try, convict, and imprison me!"

"In court?"

"Yes!"

"With laws and judges and all that?"

"YES!"

"No problem. If men are involved, I'll take care of it."

"How?"

"The old-fashioned way."

"Oh."

She snapped her teeth at me.

I thought.

"Wait! What did you mean, exactly, by 'If I win'?" I asked.

"I meant: Win and get me. Lose and go to jail."

"So that's a threat, isn't it?"

"Sure, you could think of it that way, but if you win, baby, you get your tour card thing, your freedom, and me. And we get all of the money that's coming to Bowdoin, that dirtbag. All the insurance money and all of the money he bet on you to win."

"He bet on me to win?"

"Yeah, around a million dollars. Of *my* trust money," she said. "He must have known how it would affect your game, Oozy. It must have gotten the word out and stirred up all this action."

She gave my rear another squeeze. I'd forgotten she was even in that area.

"Oh!" I said.

"Oohh, yeah, baby, we'll turn the tables on him. I'll marry you. You'll go pro. It'll be super sexy and rich and great!"

Her eyes lit up like fireballs.

"But you're threatening me!"

"Because I care about you, Oozy," she said, draping her arms over my shoulders. "Because I love you and know how well you play when you're in danger."

"This is a lot of freaking danger!"

"I know. But you eat danger for breakfast, Oozy, don't you?"

"Well …"

"Leave it all up to me," she said. "I'll take care of everything!"

"Please," I said. "Don't take care of anything!"

"And someday soon we'll be together," she said.

She snapped her teeth at me again.

"Together?" I said, with no little trepidation.

"Maybe tonight," she said, with an additional bottom squeeze.

"Tonight?"

"Tonight, Oozy, baby," she said, adding her crazy eyes. "And then we'll just see about who's celibate!"

She added a final squeeze, shivved me with another mind-freezing kiss, disentangled herself, and, in a fugue of clickity-clicks, vanished.

The Sennetts Harbor cops gave me my car keys and shoved me out of the police station. Too wired to go back to my hotel room and completely terrified that I'd find Jiggly there, I drove aimlessly around. I brooded over investigative angles I needed to cover and couldn't think of any, apart from getting back to Singer's Island. The last ferry had left, however, and there seemed no other way to get out there, short of swimming for it.

Soon, I found myself back where it all started: Sennetts Harbor itself. I parked and walked down to the pier. It was much the same. The same assortment of boats, the same twinkling lights, the same patter of drinks and conversation, the same gently rolling tide.

All of which is to say that things were very much the same as that night that Bowdoin Jones attacked me.

In the span of less than a week, I'd been attacked by two husbands, strangled, shot at, jailed twice, and (if we want to speak purely in legalities) sexually assaulted (which I kind of enjoyed, in all fairness). I took a moment to consider that my general level of anxiety had achieved a steady state. As a timely bead of cold sweat rolled from my armpit and down my side, it seemed that I was so comprehensively alarmed that there were no further degrees of alarm to explore. Indeed, it seemed like there was so much to be terrified of that all I could really do was laugh. And so I did, almost helplessly, give a little laugh.

But isn't that really how life is? Just when you've convinced yourself that you've arrived at your lowest possible ebb, that it couldn't possibly get worse, life sneaks up on you? Like some practical joker? I believe that's what Buonorotti is getting at when he talks about the goddess of golf being wrathful. The image that occurs to me is from the old MTV Jackass show, when Partyboy and a couple of the show's midgets, all in their underwear, are flying down a hill in a grocery cart. Dangerous enough, surely, but then one of their comrades runs out and improvises a new risk for the grocery cart stunt: to wit, they throw a log in front of it. Such, I'd assert, is life.

Such, at least, was my life. And the proverbial log thrown in front of my grocery cart full of midgets arrived at this very moment.

"Hey!" a voice said. "HEY! Buddy! Over here ... It's me. Bowdoin!"

I did turn around. Now my understanding of circumstances was that Bowdoin Jones was dead. The reader will recall that I had seen Bowdoin's body in the morgue less than 48 hours ago. I'd said a lot to Lunt about how maybe that lobsterman out on Singer's Island was actually Bowdoin Jones, but I didn't really believe any of that. I mean, if your boat blows up, and a charred body is produced thereof, it's probably your (that is, the boat owner's) dead body. It would require a complicated series of events to char and launch an entirely different body from your exploding boat, if you follow me.

So, my instinct here was that this was not in fact the living Bowdoin Jones talking to me. I am somewhat prone to believing in ghosts, and I did briefly consider that this was actually the ghost of Bowdoin Jones. I remember thinking fleetingly that the one thing I hadn't accounted for thus far was the supernatural. It all felt a bit Dickensian, like he was Jacob Marley and I was Ebenezer Scrooge. I'll add that the figure which addressed me was pale as a tombstone from head to toe, even his eyelids. The physical effect on me was a variety of extensions, shrivelings, impairments, declensions, as well as a general sensation of electric terror from head to toe.

"BACK!" I managed.

"It's okay, buddy, it's just me! Bowdoin Jones! I'm fine!"

"YOU'RE WHITE AS A GHOST!"

"Yeah! Funny, see I was fiddling around in the harbor house kitchen back here and a bag of flour fell on me. Dumb luck, I guess! I do suppose the whole effect may be pretty spooky and ghost-like. Anyhow, hey, listen ..."

"DON'T TOUCH ME!!"

But he'd closed and seized my shoulders. My bowels worked like a paint shaker.

"Ha! Hey! Dude? It's cool, man," Bowdoin said, kneading my shoulders so fiercely I thought they'd come apart. "I'm totally alive."

"STOP SMILING!"

"Is that not helping? Okay, is this better?"

"YES! ALIVE?"

"That's right, man. Totally alive! Easy, buddy ..."

I tentatively resumed breathing here.

"You're supposed to be dead!"

"I know. Listen, I'm sorry for running you through all this stuff. It was really my only option, and you, I'm afraid, were the easiest mark," he dropped his chin. "But I want you to know that, when it's all over, I'm gonna make it up to you."

"They're gonna convict me of your murder!"

"Ha! Yes, I know."

"HA?"

"That Jiggly! I should have known she'd figure some angle of her own to play. Where'd she scare up the body? Any idea?"

"I HAVE NO IDEA!" I barked. My volume and tonality were all over the place.

"See, Owens, it was always supposed to be a missing persons case. We didn't want to stick you with a murder."

"Great!"

"We didn't know how to anyway. Finding bodies is hard! And they kind of creep me out. Do dead bodies creep you out?"

"YES!" I said, remembering and suddenly re-alarmed. "BUT I SAW YOUR BODY AT THE MORGUE!"

"Ha. That's great!"

"Listen, Bowdoin!" I braced his shoulder now. We were sort of clutching one another like wrestlers. "You have to turn yourself in! You have to show everyone you're alive, so I don't go to jail! For murder!!"

"Damn," he said, and clicked his tongue. "Can't do it, buddy."

"CAN'T DO IT?"

"See, I'll be accused of and arrested for all these crimes."

"I've been accused and arrested for all these crimes! Like, for example, your murder!"

"Yeah, tough break, pal."

"Tough break?!"

"Listen, I've got bigger problems. I've got to find Jiggly! By the way, stay away from her. She'll play any guy for any angle, and she's capable of anything. Moreover, I'm a terribly jealous guy. I'd kill you if I thought you were, you know, *diddling* her."

He did a kind of Marty Feldman thing with his eyes. Against the powdered white hair, skin and clothes, it had a certain effect.

"OKAY!"

"You're not diddling her, are you?"

"NO!"

"Good," he said. His eyes relaxed, and he worked my shoulder a bit more. "Good! Good man! As I said, I can't find Jiggly. Do you have any idea where she is?"

"No idea!"

"She left the hotel."

"She thinks you're playing gambling and other angles that you didn't tell her about!!"

"Oh! Oh, really …"

"Yeah! I think she's angry!"

"Oh! Dang!"

"Yeah!" I said, recognizing the dread he was feeling.

"See I was supposed to lay low and stay away from her, but in the meantime, I managed to figure out a couple ways to make a bit of extra money …"

"Right, well, she felt she should have been told about that!"

"... Yeah …" Bowdoin said, trailing off.

We heard a vehicle approaching and both looked up to see a squad car cruise past the lot.

"Dang! Listen, I gotta run, Owens!" he said, as he scampered back into the bushes. "Don't worry about anything, buddy! If you go to jail … well, we'll figure it out!"

"WAIT!" I called. "Was that you who shot at me out on Singer's Island?"

"Huh! Oh, yeah! Sorry! I thought you were trying to break in!" he called back, faintly.

"On a freaking island!?"

"Sorry, buddy!" came a fainter reply.

"Sorry!?"

I heard a motor start, then saw Bowdoin in a little launch, purring out into the harbor.

I ran down the pier.

"BOWDOIN?!" I called. "WHAT IF I NEED TO FIND YOU? WHERE ARE YOU GOING? DIDN'T YOU BLOW UP YOUR HOUSE ALREADY?!"

He only waved, then vanished in the darkness. All that was left was the gentle wake of his boat, tracing a silvery path in the moonlight.

I went back to the hotel. I was desperate, or should I say, much much much more desperate than I'd been theretofore. I was entirely amped up and figured the first thing to do was tell Buonorotti that Bowdoin Jones was in fact entirely alive. I'm not sure what I expected him to do about it. In fact, his response would in all likelihood have been something like, "Have you considered the gap wedge for that depression to the left of the green on 16?"

I mean, in a sense, it was great news. The guy I was alleged to have killed was, in fact, not dead. Further, he was still out there screwing things up for me, so while the murder charge seemed like it was unraveling, it had yet to actually unravel, and Bowdoin had no intention of unraveling it any time soon, per his own words.

En route, though, I had an even more powerful reason to find Buonorotti: I'd had the idea of swapping rooms with him. That way, if Jiggly showed up, she'd have to deal with Buonorotti and his European underwear modeling ways. So, I snuck back into my room (having checked carefully for Jiggly thereabouts), grabbed my various things, hopped back in the Fury and gunned it to the Asticou Inn. Parking and marching up the steps, I realized I didn't even know what room Buonorotti was in. So, my first stop was the front desk.

"Hi! Where is Giancarlo Buonorotti's room, if you don't mind telling me?" I said, then the amps compelled me to add. "That is, tell me immediately. Now!"

"Buonorotti," the clerk hummed. "Ah, here it is, the Presidential Suite."

"Presidential Suite?"

"That's right, sir."

"Wow. Alright. Where is that, exactly?"

"It's at the very top of the hotel, sir, overlooking the ocean."

"Overlooking the ocean?"

"Is he expecting you, sir?"

"He's my caddy in this golf tournament."

"Ah, very good. May I call him and tell him you're heading up?"

"Please do!"

He did his telephoning.

"Mr. Buonorotti invites you to come right up. Just take the elevator to nine. The Presidential Suite comprises the entire ninth floor."

"The entire floor?"

"Yes, sir."

It was only then that I took a closer look at the clerk.

"Hey wait," I said. "Don't I know you from somewhere?"

"I bartend at the club. We talked about blowing up boats the other night."

"Ah, right … You guys all have like a dozen jobs."

"Many of us do, yes, sir. It's a small island."

"You're not also a Lunt, are you?"

"I'm not, sir. I'm a Jordan. Tim Jordan."

" … Well, that's great. I'll head up then."

"Very good, sir."

And so I did. The elevator pinged, the doors opened, and I took in a sweeping view of a parlor with multiple sofas and a grand piano. Buonorotti stood by the window, in which the entirety of the Atlantic Ocean glittered.

"Buonorotti! How'd you get this room?"

He looked around.

"It was the last room, Oose."

"I mean, it must cost a fortune!"

"They gave it to me at the regular rate."

"Really?"

"I was surprised, too. How may I be of assistance, Oose?"

"We've got to switch rooms. Jiggly's on the warpath. She wants to seduce, ravish and marry me! In whatever order it takes!"

"Did you tell her that you were celibate?"

"I did."

"And that you are so because it helps the golfing?"

"Yes!"

"What did she say?"

"She wasn't impressed!"

"As I would expect," he mused.

"She didn't think it could stop her anyway!"

"Your celibacy must only arouse her further."

"And I just ran into Bowdoin Jones! He's alive!"

"Really, Oose?"

"YEAH. He's also the lobsterman who shot at us out on Singer's Island?"

"Really, Oose."

"I mean he may have been a ghost, but I don't think so! I asked him! And we grabbed each other's shoulders!"

"Really, Oose?"

"YEAH," I said. "So, first, stop saying 'Really, Oose'!"

"Certainly, Oose."

"Second, I realize you have a nice set up here, but would you mind taking my room tonight and letting me have this one?"

"Of course, Oose."

"And I've got to warn you: Jiggly may try to get into that room and do you-know-what to you."

"I do know what. I will take care of it."

"Great!"

"You must have every advantage in order to play your very best tomorrow."

"Huh? Oh! Yeah!"

Buonorotti gathered his things, said something about the approach wedge, but I managed to shove him out the door and lock it behind him.

At once, the cumulative fatigue of the day began to take effect. Just for the record, said cumulative fatigue was comprised of 18 holes of professional golf, the narrow escape from the police, fisticuffs at

Beal's, gunplay at Singer's Island, a lost phone, an exploded island, a second jailing, DNA evidence, another Jiggly Jones encounter involving potential marriage thereunto, multiple tweaks of my hind-quarters, and the paranormal event with the formerly-thought-dead-but-now-very-much-alive Bowdoin Jones. All of which is to say that I was abruptly aware of my utter exhaustion and that my brain activity, modest as it is, shut down entirely.

Now of course I was still aware of the threat that Jiggly Jones posed. Previously, I'd encountered Jiggly on the club veranda and in jail. It had taken a profound exertion of will to resist her. Celibacy takes its toll, however serious one's obsession with golf. Regardless of what you've heard or read, golf is not a perfect or even sufficient substitute for sex. Further, a healthy adult male such as myself, after a protracted period of celibacy, is working with a hair trigger. You're like some kind of hyper-volatile chemical, able to be set off my the slightest kinetic, if you will, interaction with the opposite sex. And Jiggly Jones was about as kinetic as the Fourth of July. Or a hurricane! And in a very real sense, if you'll indulge the metaphor, I wanted Hurricane Jiggly to touch down in my trailer park and scatter my things a thousand miles in every direction. At the same time, she was the last thing I needed, with the final round of the tournament just a small number of hours away.

So it was with a great force of will that I remained in Buonorotti's suite, rather than reversing my decision to swap rooms. I hopped in the shower and worked the cold knob considerably, trying to cool off my jets, after which I toweled down, scrubbed dry my various sultry and nether regions, brushed my teeth, found some underwear in my golf bag, and climbed into bed. I was asleep in an instant.

I had a dream, the kind of dream that seemed inevitable under the circumstances. A pair of cold fingers slid over my loins. I pushed them away. Somehow, I knew it wasn't Jiggly, which was simultaneously a relief and disappointment. I kept sleeping. The fingers returned, traveling ever so lightly. I pushed them away again and giggled. It all seemed, in my hazy, half-awake analysis, like the perfect metaphor for my situation. Fate — or as Buonorotti might say, Golf — was teasing me, tickling me, trying to get me going. I resisted, but only faintly, and fainter still with every passing moment. Why resist? I recall thinking. It was all a dream, merely a dream, as were whatever consequences awaited me.

I heard a voice.

"Hello, dahling," it purred.

And next a pair of teeth touched my earlobe. The voice went, "Grrrr…"

I suppose it could have been the vibration in the "Grrr" that changed things initially, although I was pinched in the derriere immediately thereafter and I'll just note that Jiggly Jones had fiddled around in that region just a few hours prior. So that probably triggered certain feelings of preliminary concern. Moreover, a pinch is a sensation that's hard to merely dream. Or so it is for me. It's all a bit of blur, but suffice it to say that my dream ended abruptly, chilly sensations came alive all over, and I was shot back into reality like a cannonball.

I yelped — "Jiggly!?" — as much a meaningless cry as a name. At the same time, I sucked in a suite-full of oxygen and ascended into the air. I seemed to hover there briefly, a bit like a saint in one of those Renaissance paintings of the Ascension, then plummeted back to earth. The aforementioned fingers raced back under my clothes.

"Stop! Go! Please?! Jiggly?! No! Yes! Oh, Golf!!"

"I found you, finally, and I forgive you, dahling."

"Your fingers are freezing!"

"Ahh they?"

"Yes!"

"Come, let me varm them up."

"Please, Jiggly. Stop that silly accent!"

"Vot silly accent?"

"*That* silly accent!"

"Giancarlo, vhere has all of this hair come from, dahling?"

"Giancarlo?"

The fingers paused.

"You're not Giancarlo, ah you?"

"You're not Jiggly!?"

"Well, no matter. You can be Giancarlo tonight, yes?"

The fingers resumed, but I leapt like a spider from the bed to a chair. I flicked on a light and fluttered my eyes.

"Hello, dahling," the voice said, its source a kaleidoscope of pinks and greens.

I was shocked, naturally, to find a woman in my (or Buonorotti's) bed. However, as she came into focus, I was significantly more shocked by her brain-numbing, tongue-tying beauty. Her hair was a platinum blonde. Her eyes blue, unblinking, expectant, worldly. She wore about a thousand diamonds around her neck and little else. If Catherine Denueve had a better-looking sister, this was her!

"Who are you?" I managed.

"I am Countess Katerina de Esperantino. Who ah you?"

"I'm U.S. Owens!"

"I see. Where is Giancarlo, dahling? Why are you in his room?"

"How do you know Giancarlo?"

"He was my gigolo, of course."

"What? Oh!"

She reached for a foot long cigarette holder. She lit up, then returned her focus to me.

"Are you a gigolo as well, U.S. Owens?"

"I'm a pro golfer!"

"And also a gigolo?"

"No!"

"Well, dahling, you'll be one tonight, yes? Come here. I've had a long flight."

"Wait!" I said, "You're the Countess?"

"So," she smiled. "He told you about me."

"He said you ran off with a peasant boy!"

"It didn't work out," she said. "You are cute. A cute, little, monkey-ish, fishy-faced American boy."

"Thanks?"

"You will do fine, yes?"

She sprang like a cat, snatching up one of my big toes.

"Wait! Stop!"

"Come, come," she said around the cigarette holder. "Come here, monkey Yankee doodle boy."

"I'm celibate!"

"Ha ha ha," she said, in no way a laugh. "Let us make love, and then laugh later about these funny circumstances."

"What?"

"Let me tickle your feet …"

"No. Okay! No! Ha HA ha!"

"Touch me here, dahling."

"There?"

"Yes. Do it."

"But, Countess, I've got to golf tomorrow!"

"Did Giancarlo tell you love affects your golf game?"

Her leg slithered up mine.

"Yes!"

"He says that to everyone. He's so crasssy."

She crawled closer.

"Oh, no!"

"Oh, yes, dahling …" she purred again.

"Oh, no! No! Yes. Never! OKAY!"

At that very moment, the elevator doors pinged, we froze and a figure strode into the room.

"Oh, no!" the figure said. "I am too late!"

"BUONOROTTI!"

"Forgive me, Oose. If only I had come sooner."

"IT'S OKAY! I'M STILL CELIBATE!"

"Thank goodness, Oose."

"Giancarlo," the Countess said. "You're alive, dahling. How delightful."

"Katerina," he said. "Hello."

"And how disgraceful to your calling to run off as you did. You still owe me considerable gigolo services."

"You know that is not true. I have fulfilled my every duty."

"WHAT ARE YOU DOING HERE, BUONOROTTI!?"

"I discovered the Countess's henchmen in town, Oose. They were looking for me, and I knew at once you were in the greatest peril. I came as quickly as I could."

"Speaking of my henchmen," the Countess said, inspecting her phone. "They will be here shortly. We will review the books and see exactly what is owed."

"Katerina, we cannot go on like this."

"You keep running away."

"There are many gigolos in the world."

"Faking your own death, Giancarlo?"

"It is not you, Katerina. It is me."

"It is all beneath the dignity of ... the world's greatest lover!"

The final phrase was consumed in an explosion of tears. Indeed, ferocious tears, with a certain duration, percussive rhythm and volume. Like a hammer drill left unattended on a tin roof.

I couldn't help but look at Buonorotti.

"It is merely an expression, Oose."

"It's not merely an expression!" the Countess roared. "You are the world's greatest lover!"

Buonorotti smiled tightly at this.

"It's an award!"

"Of a kind," Buonorotti said.

"Julio Iglesias won it. And Falco!"

"Please."

"There's a trophy! With eagles and the figure of man with this incredible, gilded — "

The elevator pinged again. Two enormous men in shiny suits plowed in and began to inspect the room. A third arrived, leveling a small gun at Buonorotti.

"GUN!" I observed.

"A gun, yes, Oose. It is not a concern. These are the Countess's henchmen. Good evening, my friends."

"Show me the books," the Countess ordered, sniffling and gathering herself. "Ah! Here! Look, Giancarlo!"

She brought the book over to Buonorotti and they did some mumbling. He then held her briefly. Over her shoulder to me, he made a series of complicated frowns, a signal entirely lost in translation.

"I see, Katerina," Buonorotti said, a kind of announcement for both the henchmen and me. "It would seem I do owe you more gigoling."

"Of course you do," she sniffled.

"How can you ever forgive me?"

"Well, dahling, we'll start this evening on the plane."

"The plane?" I said.

"I'm afraid it is true, Oose. I must fly back to Esperantino tonight."

"What? Tonight?!"

"I am gigolo, Oose. I have duty."

"A gigolo duty!?"

"Precisely, Oose. I am in arrears to the Countess."

"Let's keep it clean, Buonorotti!"

"I must go, Oose."

"You cannot go, Buonorotti!" I said. "What the heck is happening here?! I mean, I've led a fairly exotic life. I wish this wasn't the first time I'd had naked women and armed men in my room simultaneously, but I have! Which I shouldn't have to tell you, Buonorotti, is not good for one's golf game!"

"Your friend here, Giancarlo, is my gigolo. I'm sure he was here with you only for the gambling."

"Gambling?"

"Katerina ..."

"He is also among the world's great gamblers, or didn't you know that?"

"She is crazy, Oose."

"Shoot him if he speaks again," the Countess said, lighting a new cigarette.

The henchmen pressed the gun into Buonorotti's gut. Buonorotti rolled his eyes.

"Let me ask you this, U.S. Owens," the Countess said. "Has he insisted you do exactly as he says?"

"Yes?"

"And has he let you make mistakes that seem of your own choosing?"

"Yes?"

"And told you there is a Goddess of Golf? For whom you must golf quietly?"

"Yes!"

"It is exactly how he tricked the many European golfers. He ... how does one say it ... yes, he *shorts* them. He bets against them. He gives them bad advice on the last day. *Voila.*"

"Are you *shorting* me, Buonorotti?"

"On my honor as a gigolo, even as a legionnaire, I am not."

"Paddington shorted me," I heard myself whisper.

"Let's go, dahling," the Countess said, crushing out her cigarette. "It's too late in the evening for such lies."

They went to the elevator. I followed. Buonorotti turned to me.

"Oose, I must go," Buonorotti said. "But know that I never gambled on you. Believe me."

"I'd like to! I don't know how I can!?"

A beat passed.

"Oose, look at me. We are golf friends. In all the world, in all the history of men and time, there is nothing more sacred than that. Golf friends do not lie to one another."

The elevator dinged its arrival. I gulped.

"But how am I going to putt?"

They stepped inside the elevator. They all turned to me. The doors began to close.

"Have a secret, quiet faith, Oose," Buonorotti said. "Let the Goddess of Golf fall asleep in your arms."

The doors had nearly shut when Buonorotti shot out a foot and stopped them with a shoe. He pointed and dropped his chin.

"And also," he said. "Do not use the naked lady tees tomorrow."

With that, the evening ended.

CHAPTER SIX — SUNDAY

As the tournament leader, I didn't start until 11:07 the next morning. From 8:00 pm until 10:00 am, I sat in my hotel room in the dark, shirtless, sleepless, weeping, laughing, fearing even the lightest wind, occasionally even doing a little karate after the fashion of Martin Sheen in Apocalypse Now.

And "apocalypse" is *le mot juste*. I knew my game would come apart faster than a Chinese motorcycle, as I once heard the great Bing Wilton describe his unraveling at Amberdon. I knew as well that I'd lost a friend: Buonorotti had been that, I realized. Of course, like most men, I only realized it in the aftermath. My denunciation of his gambling angle was ridiculous, I now saw. I mean, who am I to be taking some kind of stand on principle? I'd detonated three separate marriages! And those were just my own! Never mind all the ones I'd helped along, both as a PI and a womanizing DB! So where did I get off judging Buonorotti? And the big Italian nob didn't even have a phone! Can you judge someone so deranged? Are the standards of guilt and forgiveness even functional among the phoned and non-phoned peoples of the world?

As importantly, I needed Buonorotti's guidance. I could whang balls all over the place, but if I couldn't finish a hole in fewer than three putts, I'd be screwed. With the countless tour jocks and the freaking internet, it would be documented real-time among the great disasters in the history of sport.

At precisely 10:00 am, I dressed, took the elevator down, scanned the hotel lobby from behind a potted plant, and jogged to the Fury. Arriving at the course, I took a couple minutes on the range to check my driver and iron games. They were outrageous.

I proceeded to the practice green. Even with a half dozen holes, none more than twenty feet away, I couldn't sink anything. My reads were a house of mirrors. My putts moved around the green like beads of water on a hot skillet.

Cocky Brill was my partner and sole competition for the final round. He was announced first. He gave me a sneer and a flash of wonky, late-Empire teeth before setting his ball and drilling it.

I was announced, took in the cheers, and tipped my cap. I pushed a tee and ball into the soft earth. I took a couple waggles, eyed the fairway, released a sigh of Shakespearian intricacy, then launched Screaming Eagle into the low heavens.

The crowd roared. I took up my tee, then turned to hand them both back to the son-of-club-member who'd been nominated to carry my bag. It was then that I noticed Jiggly Jones, standing in the front row. Her sunglasses were the size of dinner plates. Her polo shirt removed any concern that she was wearing a bra. Below that, there was the fleeting implication of a skirt, but really all you saw were her perfect legs, going on almost forever, then a pair of bright white sneakers.

"Great shot, honey," she said, loudly, added a little clap, and finally did that dirty thing with her parted lips, like she was blowing the tiniest of bubbles.

I'd been mid-stride, descending the tee-box. My left knee seemed to acquire another hinge and buckled sideways, but I recovered. Jiggly did another little clap, as if to congratulate me on not falling.

My general level of fear thus goosed, my woods and iron play, if anything, improved. My putting, of course, was a day-long disaster. I would take a seven on the first hole. On the sixth, I putted across the entirety of the green three times. My lead, which started at 21, dwindled to three by the turn.

It was at that point that I managed to escape to a bathroom. I buried my face in a wet towel, then threw it over the back of my neck. That's when I heard someone enter. I didn't dare look up.

"How are ya, Owens?"

I recognized the voice. I looked up now and found Lieutenant Lunt in the mirror.

"Please tell me you're here to arrest me."

"Ha!" Lunt said, with what seemed like real pleasure. "No, I'm here to enjoy the spectacle of a first-class sports train wreck in progress."

"Great!"

"That's right. GREAT. I'm here to watch you suffer, Owens."

"Why do you dislike me so much, Lunt?"

This hit him, surprisingly. I noticed a jumpier twitch of his Captain Kangaroo mustache.

"I don't like murderers. Or arsonists."

"You know I didn't do either of those things."

"Right. And I don't like you pawing the wife of the victim."

This triggered something. My PI instincts tingled with life.

"You don't?"

"No," he answered. "I don't."

"Why not?"

"Well," he said, then seemed to have to think about it. "It's unethical."

"Is that all?"

"And, she could do better than a jerk like you," he said, adding a guffaw. "That's for damned sure!"

"Wait! Lunt! I saw Bowdoin Jones last night. He's alive!"

"Sure he is."

"I saw him down by the pier! He was the guy I thought was your cousin! Out at Singer's Island!"

"My cousin's place on Singer's Island."

"Right!"

"Sure you did," he said. "My cousin's place on Singer's Island where everything blew up right after you left?"

I gulped.

"Right!" I said.

"We were out there on the island this morning, Owens. Gathering all that evidence."

"Great!"

"We presented it to the judge about half an hour ago," Lunt continued.

"Even better!"

"He just issued your arrest warrant."

"Not as good!"

"Without bail."

"No bail?"

"You blew up an entire island, Owens," he said. "You're a threat to the community."

"Jiminy Cricket!!!"

"However, you can finish the tournament. The judge has a — what shall we call it? — a heightened interest in the outcome, knowing as he does your unique circumstances."

"So the freaking judge is gambling on me now, too?"

"But right after your epic disaster of a round is finished, Owens, your cracker ass is going to jail, and your girlfriend Jiggly ain't bailing you out this time."

"But I saw Bowdoin! You have the wrong body! You gotta ask around! Maybe somebody switched the body. No. NO! Jiggly got a body! Because that makes Bowdoin officially dead, and she gets all his stuff! Where do you get a body? Lunt?"

"Why don't you tell me, Owens? I'll bet you know."

"Well …" and here again, like a revelation, it came to me. "… a funeral home! Check the funeral home or homes around here!"

"There aren't any bodies at the funeral home, Owens. Let's go."

"How do you know, Lunt!?"

"Trust me," he said.

"Why? Does one of your cousins own the funeral home? Is it the Lunt funeral … It is. It must be!"

He didn't answer. Instead, his mustache remained perfectly, eerily still.

My PI instincts popped like fireworks.

"Is it your funeral home, Lunt?" I asked. "Do you moonlight as an undertaker? Is that your second job? Everyone works multiple jobs around here. Is that yours?"

He didn't answer.

"IT IS!"

"What a crazy idea, Owens."

"You gave Jiggly a body! Do you have a crematorium at your funeral home? Is that how you charred the body beyond recognition?"

"Ridiculous."

"But why would you do that?" I said. "Why would you produce and torch a body for Jiggly Jones unless she …"

"Right, produce and torch a body …"

At this point I gasped.

"Unless she did *Jiggly-type things* to you," I said. "She did do Jiggly-type things to you, didn't she, Lunt?"

"Let's put it this way. It'll be easy for you to stay the hell away from her when you're locked up in Maine Correctional, which is where you're going once this round is finished, Owens."

And with that, in a sudden whirlwind of emotion, he power-waddled out.

I don't remember teeing off on 10. I do remember Jiggly Jones strutting up beside me and snarling through a huge, fake smile.

"Someone just told me that your game is completely coming apart. What the hell is going on, Ooze?"

"It's my putting, Jiggly. The rest of my game is off the charts!"

"Are you going to lose?"

"Yes!"

"Which means, I think you can remember, that you lose me."

"Right!"

"And you go to jail!"

"Yes!"

"Can't you do anything about it? Can I scare you more?"

"I don't think so! What really scares me is that you apparently were *diddling* Captain Kangaroo! By which I mean, Lieutenant Lunt!"

I heard her catch her breath.

"I KNEW IT!"

"How dare you!"

She slapped me. I barely noticed.

"And I found Bowdoin, Jiggly! By the way! And he still loves you and is entirely alive!"

"You did? He does? I thought he blew up?"

"Well, he didn't."

I could tell she was thinking at a rolling boil.

"So what!" she concluded.

"So I think that complicates our marriage plans a bit, don't you? I mean between the dead body, the living husband, the various crimes and explosions!"

"If that boob, Bowdoin, is alive, I'm gonna get him. And it changes nothing!"

"Except I go to jail!"

"Well," she said, then dropped her glasses back into place. "That was the arrangement."

"That was your arrangement! I had nothing to do with it!"

Feeling a response unnecessary, she spun on a heel and strutted back into the gallery. I realized I'd arrived at my shot. She spun again, ready to watch with the others. I kept staring at her until, after adjusting her huge sunglasses again, she waggled a finger at the ball, inviting me to get on with it.

I did, bending a steep fade around some pine trees and onto the green. The crowd, as ever, roared.

And next, Cocky was at my side as we marched toward the green.

"Oy, mate? U.S.? What?" he began. "What, what, what? You're totally shagged, right? Innit? Right up the wee Black Hole of Calcutta? I mean, it's bloody looking like you might finish in the bloody 90s!"

"Yeah, Cock. Thanks to you!" I said, my PI neurons again sparkling. "You dropped the dime on us with the Countess. Your buddy recognized Buonorotti and made a call. She jumped in her jet, flew over, and whisked him away!"

"Right, I mean, that's the game, innit?" he answered, perfectly oblivious. "And as such, my original plan was to overtake you this afternoon as you got all bollixed up without your Italian gigolo green-reader. But as it happens, I'm playing even worse than you are, mate."

"Really?"

"Yeah, mate, you're all in your own litto world, ain't even noticed that I'm a plus bloody nine for the day! So anyway, there's about a billion pounds and a billion dollars and a billion bloody euros which could turn any which way, depending on how you score."

"Uh-huh."

"And old Cocky here, I'm not doing so well. Three mortgages, three ex-wives, nine kids — "

" — Nine?"

"Nine kids!" he said. "And they're all horrible little tits!"

"Jeez!"

"So I mortgaged one of the houses and put it all on you, mate," he said, clapping a claw on my shoulder as we walked.

"What?!"

"That's right," he said. "Half a million pounds!"

"Good God!"

"Quite!"

"Wasn't it already mortgaged?"

"Yeah!"

"You can do that? Mortgage a mortgage?!"

"Funny, that's what I said, that," he answered. "But my guy was like, 'Innit, right? What!' And I was like, 'Innit, what?' And he's like

'Right!' And I say, 'Hello!' He says, 'Precisely!' So I was like 'Shite in can, I want to put it all on Ooze Owens!' He's like 'Right!' and I'm like 'C'mon!' and he's like 'What!' and I'm like 'DO IT' and here we are, mate!"

"Good God!"

"It's all or nothing, U.S.," he said. "All or bloody nothing for old Cocky on one Ulysses S. Owens. And you know why I did that? Why I leveraged everything and put it all on you? You wanna know? Do you? Innit a bit, that, right? Why?"

"What?"

"Why?"

"Huh?"

"Right. Because I believe in you, U.S. Ooze! Mate! And I wanted to make it up to you for, you know, calling the Count and Countess and basically shagging you sideways," he said. "I mean I shagged you proper, right up the old balloon knot, innit?"

"That's the stupidest bet I've ever heard of!"

"Is it?" Cocky answered. "Or is it the last bet anyone ever saw coming? The important thing is, I believe you can bloody do it, mate! And you just gotta bloody believe you can do it yourself. I believe in you so much that I'm actually the bleeding bloody edge of your gambling support on this. Not even Snake Plissken is out here with me. That's how much I believe in you, US Freaking Owens!"

"Who's Snake Plissken?"

"Paddington, mate!"

"Paddington?"

"Ee's shortin' you, mate!? To the tune of $1 million, it is said."

"He shorted me at Congressional!"

"Rumor has it Paddington put this Alfred E. Newman kid on your bag."

"What?" I said. "That kid's been giving me the wrong club all afternoon!"

I turned, found and lunged for the kid, taking up most of his shirt. Cocky wrapped me up.

"Forget the kid, Ooze!" he whispered in my ear. "Forget him. He's been setting you up all day. Let me read your greens, mate!"

"You?"

"Me. Cock. My bloody life depends on it!"

"Is that even legal? You reading my greens?"

"Sure. Prolly. Why not? Oy, we're on the green already, look!"

Sure enough, we were. And Cocky, gamely, starting hopping around, squatting down, reading lines.

"Now see here, Ooze. This putt's gonna be as easy as …"

He pointed and was about to speak, when his caddy said, "Oy! OY. There's a bloody alligator in the sand trap!"

This caught everyone's attention, as one would expect, and we all sort of stopped and looked.

Now of course there are no alligators in Maine, which an Englishman can be forgiven for not knowing, so I wasn't immediately alarmed. However, I did discern a certain large-alligator-sized figure wriggling about in the sand. Fine sand poured off it as it moved, and it grew larger. Further, it did have a certain reptilian quality to its wriggling, and I recall questioning my own confidence in the habitable range of the North American alligator until the sand figure assumed the shape of a man, and then an enormous man. It stood. A mouth appeared that tried at first to yell, but was instead forced to first spit and lick away sand.

"Oooh the hell are you, mate?!" Cocky said to it.

The sand monster lumbered up from the trap, scraping sand from its eyes and approaching Cocky.

"Back the hell up, wanker!" Cocky said. "Or all whack you in the tiddly giblets, innit? What!"

The sand monster kept coming, still somewhat blind. Gamely, Cocky wound up with the club-end of his seven iron and whacked the sand monster across the midsection. It received the whack like a brick wall.

That's when everything came into focus for me.

"Jumping Jan Michael Vincent!!!" I declared to the gathered multitude. "It's Auchincloss Hastings Burr!!!"

It was undoubtedly Burr. And he could see now. Clearly the seven iron had shaken loose whatever sand remained in his eyes.

"Whoosit, now?" Cocky said, inspecting his mangled club.

"Auchincloss H. Burr!" I answered. "Run, Cocky!"

With my signature athleticism, I'd already pivoted in multiple directions, considering which way to run myself. Alas, my warning to Cocky was too late, and I saw Burr make the connection between Cocky and the seven-iron. Seizing and lifting Cocky into the air, Burr carried Cocky over his head to a water hazard, and, with a momentous boom, delivered him therein. Cocky's caddy — whether in solidarity, self-preservation, or perhaps at an instruction of Burr's that I missed — jumped into the water, too.

"He's not wearing any pants!!" someone called.

Indeed, Burr was not. Nor was he wearing anything else, merely the finest dust of sand. Two security guys raced past me and dove at him. Burr cast both into the water with almost no effort at all. Now, with a certain finality, he turned fully to me.

"Owens?" Burr said, approaching.

"Yes, Burr?"

"I'm gonna kill you now."

"Right now?"

I took up a defensive position with my golf bag — having ripped it off the back of my son-of-a-member, Alfred-E-Newman caddy. I used it like a shield, blocking two Burr's lunges until he simply reached out and tore it from my hands.

I tried a lap around the flag, then took a position behind it. Burr simply ripped it from the hole.

"Your golf flag trick won't save you this time, Owens!"

I briefly considered diving in the pond like everyone else, but Burr stood squarely in front of it. Behind me, a massive crowd and a couple other steep hazards blocked me in.

I was, in a word, defenseless.

And that's when I heard a voice from the crowd.

"Look out, Oose!"

I spun, finding a lobsterman of all things running at me, full bore. As there was no time for evasive maneuvers, I quickly went into the flamingo pose from the Karate Kid.

"Oose!" the lobsterman said, effortlessly parrying my flamingo kick, as well as my backhand karate chop. "It is me."

"Who?"

"Me! Buonorotti!"

I stopped instantly, not quite believing it. I craned my head out.

"Buonorotti?!"

He ripped off his hat to reveal his fantastic head of wavy hair.

"Buonorotti! It's you! But what about the Countess and her henchmen?"

"Didn't you get my signal, Oose? With the frowning?"

"No!"

"Allow me to explain! Aieee-EEEE!"

The last quasi-word was not in fact a part of any explanation. It should be understood, instead, as a kind of Italo-Gallic war cry. At that moment, Buonorotti shoved me out of the way. With a wheelhouse kick, he countered an Auchincloss Hastings Burr hammer blow directed toward my head.

"The frowning," Buonorotti continued over his shoulder. "Was intended to say that the Countess is crazy. That there is no choice in such situations but to do the bada-boop, and that, subsequently, I will return to help you."

"The frowning said all that?"

It should be noted that Buonorotti's wheelhouse kick had spun Burr entirely around. He quickly returned his focus to us, then to Buonorotti exclusively. They squared off.

"I also remembered," Buonorotti said, briskly. "That I paid the bail of this man, Mr. Burr. Since I thought he would also scare you."

"You did?"

"Remember? We discussed it way back when? It is no matter. I forgot, too. In any event, for your safety, I escaped from the Countess's plane, assumed the lobsterman disguise and followed you."

"Your wop bodyguard can't save you now, Owens!" Burr growled. "I've been training in Brazilian jiu jitsu for years. Ha ha ha!"

Burr got lower and did something with his fists, assuming a martial arts stance. He lifted his sandy chin and let loose his own kind of war cry. With that, he came at Buonorotti. There was a brief flurry of knuckles and heels, Buonorotti parrying each blow. Then they stepped back half a pace and began to slowly circle one other. It was instantly apparent to all that Burr and Buonorotti were both accomplished hand-to-hand fighters. A hush descended on the crowd, who, by the way, were innumerable and everywhere.

"Mr. Burr," Buonorotti said. "I am impressed with your jiu jitsu training, your size and even the traditional formalism of your nakedness, but if you persist, I must disable you."

"Ha!"

They circled.

"I will warn you one last, time," Buonorotti said. "I once fought Bruce Lee. He was, como se dice … disappointed that day."

"Yeah, right!"

"It is true. I do not wish to leave you similarly disappointed, Mr. Burr."

"Uh-huh. Hieee-OOO-Yaahh!" Burr cried and launched himself at Buonorotti.

There was another brief, pattycake-like flutter of fists. Next thing you know, Burr was spread-eagled and unconscious on the green, and Buonorotti was flicking a spot of dust from his collar.

"Thanks, Buonorotti!"

At that point, security guys zipped in from multiple directions, ganging up on Burr. Again.

"But what about the Countess and the henchmen? Won't they find out you are here and come after you?"

"Ehn. I will escape again somehow. It is more important that you play a complete tournament. Compete in a golfing sense and, Oose, in a spiritual sense. With a quiet soul."

"Right. Great!"

"Very good, Oose."

"Oh! And I solved the case, Buonorotti!"

"Very good. And what case is that, Oose?"

"The *murder* case? The murder they intend to charge me with when this is all over!"

"Yes …"

"Remember, with the morgue and the dead body and the explosion?"

"Explosion …"

"On Singer's Island? With the lobsterman? Who shot at us!?"

"Ah, yes," he said. "The murder case, with the body and the blowing up of the boat. Very good, Oose."

He'd already taken out his coursebook and disappeared into it.

"Let's go, Owens," a voice said behind us, a tour official.

I didn't dwell on the abruptness of the order. Instead, I looked to Buonorotti.

"How far back are you, Oose?"

"Eight strokes."

"You need nine birdies."

"At least."

He nodded. He looked at my putt.

"This is a birdie putt, Oose?"

"Yes."

"May I show you this line?"

"Please."

He did. I putted. I drained it.

He picked up my bag.

"Eight birdies now," he said, as the crowd, fully aware of the moment, went wild.

We roared back. I eagled 11, planting a 350 yard drive on the left edge of the green, then drilling home an angry 40-foot putt. I took pedestrian birdies on 12, 13 and 14. The crowd was enormous. White people and cocktails everywhere!

After an immaculate fade off the tee at 15, I couldn't help but say to Buonorotti.

"I can't miss!"

"You're doing well."

I handed him my driver. Emotions like live wires seem to wriggle through my veins.

"I'm not kidding," I said. "We can't be stopped. We're unstoppable!"

"Oose -"

"- Cram that in your crank hole!!!!"

"Oose, please -"

"IT'S VERY NAISE!!!"

"Oose!"

"Huh?"

"We must play within the game. With quiet souls and perfect equanimity. Yes? We must not upset the goddess."

"Yes," I said, collecting myself. "Yes, you're right. Sorry!"

"She is drowsy, but she is not entirely asleep."

"Sure! But we're killING IT!"

"Yes. Yes, is good. Open up your fists and let your hands relax."

"Right. Like this? Right?"

"Yes, and just let them fall to your side. And hang there. Gooood."

"I'm sorry, Buonorotti. I just … I just feel so good!"

"Please, US. Listen to me. Let me guide the way."

"Alright, Buonorotti," I said.

We started walking.

"What a day!" I burst, almost weeping.

"Oose, perhaps I should distract you."

"Hmm? Yes. Oh, yes! Where'd we leave off?"

"I don't remember, exactly."

"I do! You said something about living with a dozen beautiful ex-nuns?"

"Can you be more specific?"

"More specific?"

"How many ex-nuns?"

"How many beautiful ex-nuns have you lived with? They were terrorists of some kind?"

"Ah, yes."

"They wore only bandoleros …" I prompted.

"Well, I should admit that was a bit of an exaggeration …"

"When did they wear only bandoleros, Buonorotti?"

"Well, you know," Buonorotti goosed out his neck here. "Around the house, other times …"

"During the badabooping?"

"Yes," he said, garnishing it with a frown. "During the badabooping."

"Wow! WAIT! The Countess said you were the World's Greatest Lover."

He sighed.

"How is that determined, Buonorotti?"

"There is a competition …"

"A competition? For World's Greatest Lover?"

"Yes. I don't like to talk about it."

"Well you better start liking to talk about it! Are there judges? Where does it happen?"

"Oose, please."

"Is it every year?"

"Ah, we have arrived at your ball, Oose," Buonorotti said, setting the bag down.

"I want details!"

"May I remind you, Oose, that you are in grave danger."

"What's that now?"

"You may go to jail in just a few minutes. For murder. Or you may also get married to a gorgeous woman who is comfortable working with explosives and dead bodies. Yes?"

"Ah," I said, scanning, seeing both Jiggly and Lunt in the gallery. "Yes, right! Thanks, Buonorotti!"

"We will play the modest punch shot here, Oose. We have previously agreed to do so."

"Yeah, but I could also play a massive flop shot, drop it on that bump in the corner, then spin it uphill — "

" — you could do that, but would you be wooing or assaulting the goddess, Oose?"

"Hmm …"

"Such a flop shot would be as if you were pinching her bottom, Yes?"

"Yess…"

"Does one do that to a lady?"

"No?"

"Or a goddess?"

"The punch shot?"

"The punch shot, if you would, Oose."

I would and did. I putted in for an eagle.

When I took it out, Buonorotti was standing beside me, along with Cocky Brill.

"Wow! Mate, we're really doing super!" Cocky said, bobbing his bushy eyebrows at both of us.

"*We* are, Cocky?"

"Word onna street is that Snake Plissken is pissing his knickers!"

"I don't think he's even here, Cock. I haven't seen him."

"Oh, ee's here. As are most of the PGA top ten. They're walking around like a freaking boy band? All ten of them! Screaming girls everywhere! And people are like, 'Oy, is that One Direction? Is that One D? Is it? Nah, it's just Biff Furlong. Justin Plunk. Henvik Stencil. Paddy Fitzsnacklesvy. Roos Vuizenheuven. Hamburg de Gerhardt. Ishu Mushumishi. Tim Smith.' All in bloody shorts!"

"We are due at the next tee, gentlemen," Buonorotti said.

"Say, mate," Cocky pointed at Buonorotti. "What you got ridin' on this, then?"

"I am not gambling."

"C'mon!"

"Is true."

"Right!" Cocky laughed out loud. Another thought, however, seemed to supersede that one and scrunch up his nose. Cocky looked furtively about, then leaned in. "You in on this alleged catfight action?"

"Catfight?" Buonorotti said.

"Catfight, friend. A nod's as good as a wink."

"Of this I know nothing."

"Well. Seems to be reserved for the cognoscenti, then, don't it?" Cocky said. "In fact, no one knows who said catfight involves. Just supposed to happen here. Momentarily, as it were. Extremely randy, of course."

"A catfight? In the middle of pro tournament. That's ridiculous, Cocky."

"And yet, it happens all the time on the Euro tour."

"What? Where?"

"Well, the semi-pro Euro tours, of course. Semi-pro, southeastern Euro tour? Like, the Transylvanian semi-pro tour? Happens all the bloody time! Kind of a lingering gypsy thing, innit? What? Golfing over here, catfighting over there, major gambling everywhere. Very, *very* randy entertainment, mate," Cocky sniffed conclusively.

At that point, thankfully, Cocky was called away to hit a shot.

"How completely ridiculous," I said. "Organized catfighting at a professional golf tournament."

"It is a strange world," Buonorotti observed. "If you would, Oose, I think you should play faster."

"Sure. Why?"

"I fear the Countess, now that I am without my own disguise, will find me here and send her henchmen," he spoke into the distance. "Perhaps this time, they will have orders to kill me."

"Why?"

"So that no one else may ever … have me, Oose."

"I had no idea it was so hard being the World's Greatest Lover, Buonorotti!"

"It is sad and ironic, in that regard," he said. "But I have planned for such a possibility."

"Planned what, Buonorotti?"

"It is better that you do not know, Oose," he said, then cast an eye over the shimmering fairway. "Let us merely play faster and hope that the goddess herself is not awakened by our haste."

And we did play faster. On the tee at 16 Buonorotti set up my ball. He'd barely stepped away when I just walked up, waggled the club mid-stride, then drew it back. I was so limber my shoulders torqued in one direction while my hips de-torqued in the other, like a freaking gimbal set. It seemed like an eternity before my hands fell. When they finally did, it was with a scandalous, filthy load of lag, not unlike a car in a slow-motion crash test plowing into a wall. My hands chased the ball off the tee. The club reached out at it. The tee tumbled through the air, the ball itself rising, rising still, then pixelating in the hard blue sky.

I drew it only slightly, like casting a fly in a faint wind. It soared fifty feet over the hazards, 340, 350, 360 and then, PLANK, it caught a sprinkler head and bounded into the sky again, but still dead on target. It dropped and rolled another five feet to lie, as God is my witness, eight inches from the hole. In 30 years of golf, it was the greatest shot I ever hit, saw hit, read about being hit, or even heard of having been hit. It went 410 yards. I tapped in 16 with an eagle.

It was the same story on 17: a massive drive, a towering approach, Buonorotti read it, and I putted in for birdie.

I was 13-under going into 18. I didn't stop. I was too terrified to even consider stopping. I drove Screaming Eagle through a new gap in the trees, then faded it. I hit a lob wedge up, leaving a 30-foot putt.

Looking over the green, I could see that Screaming Eagle rested at the peak of a ridge, barely holding on. I didn't dare approach it, even as the crowd howled and bayed.

"So what do I have on the card, Buonorotti?"

"You have a 56, Oose," he said. "A 56."

"A 56?"

"A 56. Is good."

If I made it, I'd finish with a 57. In the history of recorded professional golf, no one has shot a 57. Three guys shot a 58. A couple dozen, a 59.

"So where's my line, Buonorotti?"

But he didn't answer.

I turned. I looked at him. All I saw were mirrors.

"Where's my line?"

"I do not know, Oose."

"You don't know? How can you not know?"

"I don't know. You know. Only you know. You will putt yourself for a 57. With a quiet soul."

"Now, listen, Buonorotti," I said, feeling myself steam up. "I don't have time to fool around right now. Show me my line!"

"No."

"SHOW ME."

"I will not, Oose."

"BUONOROTTI."

"As a golf friend, Oose —"

"RYAN FREAKING SEACREST ON A POSTAGE STAMP!"

" — I believe you can make this putt, Oose."

"BUONOROTTI!" I began, managing to muzzle myself slightly. "If you don't show me that freaking line right freaking now — "

I didn't finish. I wanted to, and had a complete thought, but was totally cut off by the enormous sound of perhaps a dozen car doors slamming simultaneously, like an artillery barrage.

I spun to see huge men in shiny suits coming our way. Swarthy men, with beards and muscles. And they kept coming, spilling out of SUVs like a clown car act!

"The henchmen are here, Buonorotti!"

"Is okay, Oose. Please, putt."

"There's a crapload of them, too!"

"Be quiet in your soul, my friend."

And then, from the last SUV, the Countess hopped out, hitting the ground running. On heels! Though gorgeous, she was also, somehow, angrier than her henchmen.

"The Countess is here, too!"

"I know. It is okay. It is part of the plan."

With that, Buonorotti snapped his fingers. A sound like a Comanche war party galloping downhill filled the atmosphere to my immediate right: a couple dozen big guys in tight shirts came rolling over a hill.

"Who are these guys, Buonorotti?!"

"Eh, they are … gambling enthusiasts, Oose."

The big guys collided with the henchman like something out of Braveheart. Fists and teeth and arms and elbows everywhere.

"And they're part of the plan, Buonorotti?"

"I will explain later, Oose. Please, I must insist you putt now."

"Gambling enthusiasts?"

"And underworld types, yes," he said, taking my arm and redirecting me to my ball. "You must putt now, Oose. Show yourself the line. There is nothing else but that."

I heard the crescendo of irate, female Italian as the Countess curled around the battling goons, speed-strutting over the lawn towards us. She whipped a finger in the air, and instantly a new squad of henchmen appeared from the left.

"Excuse me, Oose," I heard Buonorotti say, and at once he stepped away and engaged this new platoon of henchmen. Single-handedly!

Next and inexplicably, the Countess seized Jiggly Jones from the gallery and spun her around. I'd almost forgotten Jiggly was even there!

Jiggly was surprised herself. The Countess rattled off something nasty in Italian, though it would have been understandable in its fundamentals in any language. Certainly Jiggly understood, as she was instantly defiant and welcoming of the confrontation.

"I don't know who your man is, Euro-ho," Jiggly observed. "But maybe *he* should stay away from *me*!"

She also did a snake-like, Beyonce-esque, *no-you-dint* thing with her finger and head. Unimpressed, the Countess punched Jiggly in the mouth. Briefly stunned, Jiggly recovered, seized a fistful of the Countess's hair, and cranked it.

"Puttana!!" the Countess howled, rotating and arching backwards.

"Skank!!" Jiggly countered.

"CATFIGHT!" someone somewhere shouted.

"Putt, Oose!" I heard Buonorotti call. "Your soul is quiet now, despite all this. You can do it!"

I knew at once that he was right. I stood in a roiling sea of deranged humanity, and I was unfazed! It meant nothing! The fear, despite everything, was gone. I looked down at my putt, and the line appeared like the freaking yellow brick road! A gentle 20-foot lean left with an eight on the stimp!

"I can see it, Buonorotti! I can see the line!"

"Good!" he called from the din. "Putt!"

I set down Screaming Eagle. I took an enormous breath. I wiggled my toes. I took a deep breath. I putted.

I barely touched it, but Screaming Eagle took off, accelerating along a gentle descent, wobbling briefly atop a little hill, then falling starboard, right on target. Dead on. Unstoppable!

Meanwhile, the chaos continued unabated. A half-dozen men ran past me — in front, behind, my ball disappearing in the blur. The last guy hit me like a hockey check, but we both managed to stay upright.

"Which way to the catfight?!" he gasped.

"Outta the way!?" I countered.

He snorted dismissively, looked around, then threw himself into a nearby crowd like he was diving into a mosh pit.

I looked. The green, moments ago, had been filled with running men — now it was totally empty.

"It's gone, Buonorotti!"

My first thought: someone took it! Someone kicked it! One of these galloping country club reach-arounders squashed it an inch into the turf! There were people everywhere!

My head snapped to Buonorotti.

"Look in the hole, Oose!" he answered, even as he headlocked one henchman and kicked another in the ear.

I gasped. I'd looked everywhere else!

I approached. The flag lay inert and miserable beside the yawning hole. I looked down.

"Is it there, Oose?!"

My own shadow obscured everything. I saw only an abyss. I crouched lower. I reached in.

"Is it there?!" Buonorotti cried.

My fingers hunted.

"Oose?!"

I felt something. I pulled it up.

And there it was: Screaming Eagle.

"It was in the hole," I heard myself whisper.

I stood, turned and showed Buonorotti, almost not believing it myself. He looked, smiled and gave me a frown-plus-thumbs up, even as he parried more fists and kicks.

That's when Lieutenant Lunt stepped directly between us, wearing his fully self-satisfied smirk.

"Looks like your tournament and really your life as a free man are over, Owens," he said. "Congratulations on the win, though."

With that, his men seized me. They took my wrists, pulled them behind my back and cuffed me up.

"Let's go," Lunt said.

The henchmen and gambling goons were still slugging it out to the left, so Lunt steered us right. Here another battle raged, set smack in the middle of the clubhouse lawn: a full-on catfight between the Countess and Jiggly. Their scanty clothes, amidst all the raking and gauging, had gotten significantly scantier, which seemed to be the focus of well-organized gambling action. Bets and shouts and slurs moved among the crowd like the pit at the NYSE. Lunt, wanting to avoid and/ or ignore whatever crimes this involved, turned us another 90 degrees. There, Buonorotti threw jabs and roundhouse kicks among his remaining henchmen. Thus, we were effectively surrounded by three different arenas of violence. In fact, the action was collapsing on us. The air tingled like a riot. A music of cackles, shrieks and jeers rose from every corner. It was, in the formal sense of the term, pandemonium.

Then, someone shot a gun.

Everyone instantly froze. My first thought was that it came from one of these Sennetts Island cops. However, their guns were still holstered, and their hands were fully occupied manhandling me. Lunt himself didn't even have a gun. Looking up, my eyes raced to find the source. Everyone's did.

And we all found it.

It was Wink Paddington.

He held a smoking revolver in the air and wore that signature "I don't know what's going on but I like it" smile.

There was a short moment while we all did a bit of processing. I locked eyes with Auchincloss Hastings Burr, who was himself a bit surprised. Not enough, though, to miss the opportunity at hand. With a blink of realization, he shrugged off two security people and bolted. It says something about the moment that Burr was barely noticed, an enormous naked man streaking away down the fairway on the 9th.

"I apologize for the gun fire everybody," Paddington said, tucking the revolver in the back of his shorts. "That seemed like the only way to cool things down."

He did a kind of shrug here. There was light, strange, nervous-because-he's-a-celebrity laughter.

"The state police have been called. So, if you're concerned with being arrested or have any kind of criminal past, please consider this fair-warning," Paddington called out.

This had an effect, particularly on the gambling enthusiasts, who seemed to sulk away. Slowly, the tension dissipated. Paddington waited as it did so, smiling patiently at the gallery.

"We can't have this sort of thing at a place as nice as the Sutton Harbor Club," he said to them.

There were a couple light, unplaceable harumpfs.

A voice ventured, "Is that gun loaded, Wink?"

"Well, there's no point in an unloaded gun."

This seemed to embolden others. Questions came in quick succession.

"What kind of gun it?"

"It's a .38, right, Mr. Paddington?"

"It is a .38, yes."

"How'd you get in with it?"

"Weren't you frisked outside the club? Everyone was frisked."

"Even these goons were frisked!"

"He's Wink Paddington. He doesn't get *frisked*!"

"Have you killed anyone, Wink?"

"Where are those bullets gonna land?"

"Is Tiger here?"

Paddington raised his hands.

"First of all, I'd like to say that these are all good, important questions," he said. "However, things have calmed down a bit, so I'd like to get back what I originally wanted to say."

"Which was, Wink?"

"Something truly extraordinary just happened. In 2003, Ernie Els shot a 31-under to win the Mercedes Championship. Up to that moment, it was the greatest tournament performance in the modern era. The lowest 72-hole score to par ever. But with his putt, just a moment ago, U.S. Owens here beat that score."

"Wow, Wink!"

"That's right," Paddington said. "Wow. And it happened right here. For the sake of the game. For the sake of sports and, frankly, because it seems like Owens is about to go to jail, I'd like to take a moment to acknowledge his incredible accomplishment."

With that, he started clapping. Others joined in and pretty soon the entire crowd cheered. I'll admit, I was touched, despite the circumstances.

Amidst the fanfare, Paddington crossed over to me and the Sennetts Harbor cops. He took my arm. The cop holding me shot a look at Lunt. The crowd noticed, however, and was electrified. Lunt, inadequate to the moment, quickly nodded his acceptance.

Seeing us together, the crowd went wild. At some point Paddington waved, trying to calm them down.

"Don't make me shoot my gun again!" he called out, and manic laughter combined with the general fanfare to create an Altamont-esque atmosphere of total insanity. I think Paddington did actually fire off a couple additional rounds, this time largely for fun. He certainly had that huge smile on his face.

In any event, someone slapped me on the ass, and that kind of brought me back to reality.

"But I'm innocent, Wink," I said, turning to him.

"What's this, Oscar?" he answered, tucking the gun away again. It was a bit hard to hear over the crowd.

"I'm innocent."

Paddington seemed to hear me this time. He shrugged as if it were at least a possibility and started to quiet the crowd.

"I mean, I'm really innocent," I repeated, when the volume had dropped enough.

The crowd seemed to take this as a joke, returning a light laugh.

"How exactly do you mean, Oscar?"

"It's Ooze, Wink, not Oscar," I said. "And I mean I didn't do it."

With impeccable timing, Buonorotti appeared in front of us. In his arms he held a sheepish, black-eyed Bowdoin Jones. Buonorotti gave me a double frown.

"The guy I was supposed to have murdered is actually right there," I said, pointing.

"Really?" Paddington said.

"Really," I said. "Yeah, that's him. Bowdoin Jones. That's his wife there, splayed out on the green. Her name is Jiggly Jones."

"Wow, is that right?"

"It is," I said, then faced Lieutenant Lunt. "Isn't it, Lunt?"

He resisted, but eventually gave a nod.

"Well," Paddington said, sort of looking around. "No one's arresting you now, Ooze. Not with these two here alive and kicking, as I believe you say in the lobster business."

There was another eruption of outsized laughter — someone briefly attempted a *Lock him up! Lock him up!* cheer — but Paddington reigned it all in.

"Now, now," he said. "It wasn't that funny … Okay, maybe it was. In any event, Ooze, you have to tell us what happened here."

He invited the crowd, with just a few hand gestures, to form a neat half circle around me, and they did. They were murmuring, whispering, making hushed remarks. Some glowered, others beamed, presumably according to their gambling fates.

"U.S.?" the unplaceable voice from the crowd called.

"Yes?" I answered, just as my hands fell free from the cuffs behind me.

"What happened?"

"Well …" I began, and held them spellbound for at least five minutes.

I can't recall verbatim what I said, though it was dynamite.

"I believe it was Wellington who said, of Waterloo, that it was a 'damned close run thing,'" I began. "In many respects, if not all, that was exactly the case here. So here's what happened. Mr. Bowdoin Jones got in some deep shinola with his massively leveraged investments and businesses and entities, etc., or so I would guess. Some sort of huge financial swindle. He figured he couldn't pay his debts legally, so in the long tradition of shifty financiers, he elected to disappear. He and Mrs. Jones worked up this plan where they would fake his death. Somehow they'd heard about me, a professional golfer who also solved crimes. They figured, because Mrs. Jones was so hot, they could say I fell hard for her, then decided to bump off Bowdoin in a big boat explosion. Simple enough. So, they set me up. The boat explodes. Mr. Jones disappears. Mrs. Jones humps my leg a bit to get me to do what she wants. They feel pretty good about it, since, without a body, I won't actually be accused of murder and as such probably won't get in nearly as much trouble. Quite considerate. But then Mr. Jones learned that my playing could generate significant gambling interest. He tried to get in on that, but didn't tell his wife. This made her very angry, inspiring Mrs. Jones to produce a body for her husband. That way she'd inherit all of her husband's money and generally create lots of significant new problems for him, inasmuch as he'd be officially, legally dead. With that in mind, she bedded a local cop who moonlights as the town undertaker. That guy right there: Lieutenant Bob Lunt."

I pointed *j'accuse* style. Up to that moment, Lunt had been hanging on my every word, wearing an expression of beatific innocence. When the crowd zoomed in on him, however, he woke up, gave a little hop, then ran for it. Buonorotti extended a helpful foot, tripping Lunt and sending him aerially into a big boxwood.

"Yes, there, that's him," I said. "Please, if you would? Just hold him here? Yes. Great. So Mrs. Jones and Lieutenant Lunt produce a body. They just grab the freshest stiff at the funeral home. Lunt torches it in his cremator, making it look damaged by the explosion as well as generally unrecognizable. He throws it in the ocean, and when it washes ashore, he declares that it's Bowdoin Jones. Right? Everyone with me?"

We paused here for a few questions.

"Who blew up the other boats?"

"Bowdoin did. He probably took a cut of the insurance payout."

"Where'd he learn to do that?"

"Well, he actually had a local lobsterman, whom he later impersonated, show him how."

"How'd that guy know?"

"All boat owners, sooner or later, think very seriously about blowing up their boats."

"Why couldn't Jiggly and Bowdoin get back together and clear this all up?"

Bowdoin, apparently enjoying the spotlight, decided to answer this one.

"Well, it was mostly a communications issue at first. I thought I was supposed to remain in hiding. Then, when Jiggly got mad at me, she went into hiding herself and I couldn't find her."

Some oohs and ahhs followed.

"Where'd she hide?" an old lady asked.

"The funeral home," Bowdoin answered. "I'm afraid of dead bodies, which she knew, naturally, being my wife."

"So no one's dead?" somebody asked.

"No new people are dead, that's correct," I said. "We've just had a garden variety incident of massive fraud."

More oohs, ahhs, and a wow. A slow clap grew into a sizable ovation for yours truly.

"Thank you," I said a few times, faintly trying to suppress the adulation. "Thank you very much."

Jiggly Jones wobbled into the frame, bereft of one very high heel and much of her clothing. Bowdoin, who had apparently been quite enjoying himself up to that point, saw her. Clearly stunned by her post-catfight state, he cratered emotionally. She, in turn, collapsed in his arms. There was a blubbery exchange of tears, apologies, reaffirmed love, and could-you-ever-forgive-mes. Immediately thereafter, solemn promises were made to never again exclude one another from any gaming, blackmailing, sailing, banking, extra-legal or extra-marital schemes. The crowd was touched, offering another light round of applause that the Joneses took with weepy nods and becoming grace.

"Gosh, that's nice," Paddington said. "Be that as it may, perhaps the remaining Sennetts Harbor cops should take these two in? Seem like a good idea? Great."

With admirable promptness, the remaining Sennetts Harbor cops cuffed up Bowdoin and Jiggly.

"So sorry, Oose, buddy," Bowdoin quivered, encouraged by an equally quivery Jiggy. Then he raised his voice to the crowd. "Don't worry, everybody! We're still loaded and can beat these charges in any court in the nation!"

I think he expected a bigger reaction, but they were merely hauled off to the squad car.

"Who were those people, Oose?" I heard at my elbow.

"Buonorotti! You're okay? Great!" I said, then heard him. "That was Bowdoin and Jiggly Jones!"

He frowned, then seemed to look more closely at them.

I said, "I thought you grabbed Bowdoin just now because you knew I was accused of his murder?"

"Murder, Oose?"

"Yeah!"

"No. He tried to interfere with the catfight."

"Because his wife was *in* the catfight! He must have been following her around the course, since he's crazy jealous."

"His wife is Jiggly?"

"YES. The Joneses! The people who tried to frame me!"

"I see. Well, it's good they've been arrested."

"Remember Jiggly Jones?"

"Sure, I do …"

"… Forget it! What happened to all the Countess's henchmen?" I asked, noting their absence.

"I took care of a few. The Gambling Enthusiasts had done most of the work. Uh-oh, Oose."

Buonorotti redirected my attention. I saw the tour official approach Paddington and whisper in his ear. There was an indication of shock, more whisperings, some shrugs, and there it ended. Of course, I knew something was up.

"Ladies and gentlemen," Paddington began. "Ladies and gentlemen, I'm afraid there's a new development … Ron? Ron Lunt, right? Can you explain things here? As I understand it, there's some kind of a rules issue, Ron?"

Ron cleared his throat and began.

"It's really a rather minor rules issue," he pushed some reading glasses higher on his nose and read from a print-out. "But it is nevertheless an issue of tournament golf. That last putt — "

" — and what a sensational putt it was," Paddington interrupted. "Like 40 feet or something! With all those crazy breaks?"

" — that last putt," Ron continued. "Was impermissible under our tournament rules due to the fact that numerous non-tournament personnel were on the course and in the field of play. Specifically, various club staff, golf fans, policemen, underworld types, mercenaries, and lesser nobility were in fact on the green during the shot itself."

"What?!"

"Che cosa?"

"Tough break, Oscar!"

"The good news is," Ron said, removing the glasses now. "You can replay that stroke, Mr. Owens."

"Hey, great!" Paddington said, giving my shoulder a squeeze. "Good for you, Owens. I mean, you're locked in today. And now, with all this murder stuff behind you, you've got nothing to worry about. Nothing at all!"

He gave me that smile. I swear — I swear on a stack of holy Bibles — that there was something deeply sinister in that big, sunny, Californian smile of his.

"Who here thinks Owens can drain this putt?" he said, starting to clap again. "Because I know he can! Yeah. Yeah!!"

And then everyone was cheering like maniacs once more. And next Wink Paddington was escorting me back to the putt. Someone had even put a marker down. It read quite clearly "W.K.P." in gold lettering on a silver outline.

"Wendell Kneiss Paddington," Paddington whispered to me, giving my shoulder yet another squeeze, picking up his marker and putting Screaming Eagle down.

"I believe in you, Oscar," he whispered.

There was a glimmer of that smile, then his silhouette against a white hot sun, then he was gone.

I was left standing over the ball. Buonorotti, appearing out of nowhere, handed me the putter.

"Oose …" Buonorotti said. "I am happy to show you the line now."

I looked up at the heavens. I sighed.

"Forget it, Buonorotti," I answered. "I already played the round that mattered. I already made golf history. Thank you, my friend, for all your help. I couldn't have done it without you."

"Thank you, Oose, for reminding me of the beauty of this game."

We stood for a moment in perfect silence.

I clicked my tongue, resigned myself to fate, and, with that, stroked the putt.

I caught it flush — as flush as any putt I've ever hit — and away it rolled. I straightened to watch. I would be lying if I said I didn't feel a certain affection for that ball. Screaming Eagle seemed to run away, as if animated, with a kind of child-like purpose and urgency. It rolled through golden sunlight and pools of shadow. It hopped over some imperfection in the grass, seemed to shudder, then recovered its line with even more determination.

"Go!" people called.

"Get home!"

"Do it!"

"Get in the hole!"

It wasn't a 40-foot putt. It was more like 60, but I had the line dead cold. Screaming Eagle climbed at just the right rate, then banked just the right amount left, then began a precipitous, but precise descent. The line was instantly clear to everyone. A charge of energy pulsed through the crowd.

"GETINTHEFREAAKINGHOLE!!"

Screaming Eagle rolled faster, brimming with confidence.

10 feet.

Five.

The sun briefly dimmed, darkened, then returned brighter, showing Screaming Eagle ride the curl of the cup edge.

"AAAIIEEEEEEEEEEE!"

A full revolution. You could hear it, a needle at the edge of a record.

"OOHHHMYGOODDD!!!!!!!!!!!!!!"

The sun flared, like a bad bulb, and threw down a million pinions of extra, useless light. Screaming Eagle was a mirror ball.

"C'MON YOU M'ER EFER!!!""

A second spin. A third! Would it even stop?

"C'MONNNNN!!!!"

"DOOITTTT!!!!"

"SWEETJEHOVAHINHEAVENPLEASE!!!!!!!!"

And it scooted out.

It scooted, stopped and sat there, perhaps 16 inches from the hole. Only the breeze moved.

For a brief moment, in the blazing sunlight, no one spoke. I'd be significantly over my skis if I suggested that we all, again briefly, felt a certain collective pathos, if that's the word I want. I will at least say that we all looked at one another and didn't really want to know what the other was thinking. Also, I don't think I was the only one who thought that Screaming Eagle was — again for just a fleeting moment — a stupid little ball. And further, that I was stupid little man, surrounded by stupid little people, and together we were a stupid little tribe in a stupid little corner of a cold, vast cosmos, endlessly expanding in its heartless stupidity. As a series of thoughts goes, it gives one pause.

But that passed, overwhelmed by a sudden avalanche of extreme, starkly polarized, entirely genuine gambling emotion. The invocations of triumphant, fist-shaking winners. The wailing profanities of teeth-grinding losers. I saw shattered women and hysterical children. Fat cats throwing arms around one another. Other fat cats importuning the heavens like something out of the Old Testament. Among them all, like a saint, I saw Paddington, his lips tight, his focus on me, wearing an expression of genuine sympathy, even solidarity, until he too was enveloped in the chaos.

I walked up to my remaining putt and tapped it in amid the tumult. Buonorotti took up Screaming Eagle and replaced the flag. He handed me the ball and shook my hand.

"A brilliant round, Oose, by any standard."

Then, I felt the tumult approach. We both turned. A small, fat guy in a pink shirt faced us. He had a kind of anxious energy that made him seem like he burned off a thousand calories just standing still. Another couple guys, none of whom were meaningfully different than this first guy, joined him.

The first guy maintained his rolling boil for a moment, then reached into his pocket and pulled out a wad of cash about the size of a volleyball. He said something in a mysterious language, then handed Buonorotti the whole wad, and not without a certain postpartum emotion. Then the other guys did the same.

"I bet on the catfight, Oose," Buonorotti said, reading my reaction.

"Between Jiggly and the Countess?"

"Mrs. Jones, as an amateur, is very promising, but the Countess is an accomplished and gifted catfighter of some renown in Catalonia. It was always going to end as it did, with the Countess winning."

The gaggle of catfight losers finished giving Buonorotti money and scurried off.

"So you knew about the catfight? About this whole catfight thing?"

"Ehn, I actually arranged the catfight. I left a note on my pillow telling the Countess I was hopelessly in love with one Jiggly Jones."

"What?!"

"I saw the possibility of a notable catfight several days ago," Buonorotti said, watching the gamblers depart. "Mrs. Jones is a sexy, crazy, combative woman, a natural catfighter if ever I have seen one. I knew the Countess, having read the note, would be here at any moment, and she is among the most accomplished catfighters in the world. Underground catfighting is very big, Oose. I, in fact, managed a team of catfighters in Bucharest for a number of years. I put the word out through the caddy catfighting network, which was easy with all of the European golfers here."

"You were like the Don King of European Catfighting, you're saying?"

"It is a highly esteemed sport in many parts of the world."

"Are you going to tell me you lived with — and badabooped — your own team of catfighters in Bucharest, Buonorotti?"

"The badabooping was an important part of the training, Oose."

"Wow!"

"In much of the world, this is an expected duty of a gigolo. Training catfighters and organizing catfighting events such as this."

"Where'd you get the money to gamble in the first place?"

"I bet your car, Oose," Buonorotti said.

"WHAT?!"

A shadow appeared beside us.

"Excuse me? Oscar?"

We both turned to find Paddington smiling, and taking his hat off.

"Yes?" I said, with a light sneer. "*Wink.*"

"I'm going to take off momentarily. I just wanted to congratulate you once more, privately, on one of the greatest rounds of golf I've ever seen."

"Well. Thanks."

We shook hands. He changed focus.

"You're Buonorotti, aren't you?"

"I am."

They shook.

"I thought so," Paddington said. He raised his chin ever so slightly. "Was this catfight your operation?"

"It was."

"It was a good show."

"Thank you."

"Pretty euro, but I made a little money on it, too," Paddington said. "So you know."

"I'm glad that you did. That is what a good catfight is for."

"Uh-huh," Paddington answered, gave a flicker of a smile, then said. "It's been a long time since Aberdeen."

"It has, and yet I think we will meet again."

Like a genie materializing from thin air, the Countess herself appeared. Just as suddenly, her retinue surrounded us. She narrowed her eyes at Buonorotti.

"My compliments, dahling, on the catfight contest you arranged," she said, though it sounded like a death sentence. "Did you ever truly love that woman, as you claimed?"

"I did not, Katerina. I needed to distract you, so I could help Oose finish his golf."

"And gamble and make some money, too, Giancarlo."

"It was an incidental outcome."

"And saying you were tired after the badaboop, pretending to fall asleep, then arranging the scrunched up pillows under the blanket on the plane in the shape of a body — a very clever ruse."

"I am sorry to have deceived you, Katerina."

"In any event, you come with me now," she raised a lip. "You cannot run. I talked to a big-shot, state-court judge who happened to be observing the catfight. I explained that you may have overstayed your visa. At first he was unconcerned. Then I explained that you were a criminal and crazy terrorist person. He was unimpressed. Then I said I heard you speak admiringly of Donald Trump, and the judge sprung into action! INS policepeople will be here at any moment!"

Buonorotti shot me a look.

"But, I need him, Countess," I said. "For golf!"

"I need him, too," she answered, without looking at me. "For the oldest reason there is."

"Taxes?"

"The badabooping."

"It is a great honor to be in the presence of the Countess of Esperantino," Paddington interjected. "My name's Wink Paddington."

He extended a hand. Abruptly, the focus of everyone swung to Paddington and his hand. The focus of everyone but the Countess, that is. In the distance, an American flag flapped in the wind.

No one spoke.

"*The* Wink Paddington," he added.

"The golfer," I contributed. "Who I almost beat at the U.S. Open at Congressional in — "

"Hhsstt," Countess countered, apparently an order to zip it.

"I have to say, I've never met a Countess," Paddington persevered. "Are they all as lovely as you?"

Her eyes, locked on Buonorotti, eventually slid to Paddington. Meanwhile, he set his glare and smile on me, and for an eerily long moment. I realized, almost too late, that it was a signal.

"No," the Countess answered him. "Most countesses are ugly, overbred dogs."

"Ha ha ha!" Paddington responded, as did his own retinue and eventually even that of the Countess. When the volume reached a certain point, Paddington added, "Ha ha ha! Run, Oscar!"

Paddington took the Countess in both arms, spun, dipped, and kissed her. Buonorotti bolted instantly. I was temporarily paralyzed.

I came to my senses, however, when Paddington's people tangled up with the Countess's henchmen. I ran like heck for the Fury, which Buonorotti brought to skidding stop in front of me.

Somewhere on I-95, we started talking again.

"The Demon Goddess of Golf, Buonorotti," I said, with a certain mystic vision. "She is a gorgeous countess. With henchman. A castle. And a jet!"

"And, Oose, an insatiable appetite for the badabooping."

"That was her, wasn't it?"

"It was. And it was also Jiggly Jones, Oose," he answered. "With her schemes and temper and beauty."

"And low regard for underwear!"

"How dangerous these demons are."

"We were lucky to survive, Buonorotti!"

"Bad luck, borne nobly, is good luck, Oose."

"Good line, Buonorotti. Yours?"

"Marcus Aurelius."

"The cornerback?"

"The emperor, Oose."

THE END

ABOUT THE AUTHOR

Jack Howland's fiction has been featured in *The Mississippi Review*, *The American Spectator* and <u>The Best American Mystery Stories</u> series. He grew up in Chicago, where he worked as a bartender, writer and improv performer. Currently, he lives and works in Boston.

Read more from and about the author at jackhowland.com.

Made in the USA
Middletown, DE
28 May 2022

66336957R00154